Her Master Key

Shruti Johri has published newspaper columns, blogs and short stories. She is among the top ten winning writers at *The Times of India* - #TOIWriteIndia.

This is her first book.

She is an instructional designer, trainer and researcher by profession. Her career started with hotels where she gained most of her work and life skills.

Shruti is married and has two daughters.

Follow Shruti on:

Twitter @shruti_johri

Facebook www.facebook.com/shrutijohri

www.shrutijohri.com

Advance praises:

Her Master Key is entertaining and thought provoking! It unfurls the lesser known world of hotel housekeepers for us.

—*Tuhin A. Sinha,*
Author

For someone who has spent a lot of his life in hotel rooms, I have always wondered why hoteliers do not write their stories. They see, hear and know so much. I have spoken to some of them about this and they are all so quick to swear by an unwritten code that forbids them to do so. In that context, Shruti's work is very praiseworthy and valuable. She is authentic, engaging, thought provoking, funny. But in all this, there is an underlying theme of humanity in the sights and sounds and smells she weaves. This is a good read!

—*Subroto Bagchi,*
Indian Entrepreneur and Business Leader

Having been in Hospitality for over two decades, reading the book was like living my hotel life all over again. I realized that there is no better school for understanding human behaviour than hotels. Brilliant work by a brilliant senior of mine from college!

—*Ranveer Brar,*
Chef and Food Stylist

Her Master Key

A Hotel Housekeeper's
Stories from Inn-dia

SHRUTI JOHRI

Published by
Rupa Publications India Pvt. Ltd 2017
7/16, Ansari Road, Daryaganj
New Delhi 110002

Sales Centres:
Allahabad Bengaluru Chennai
Hyderabad Jaipur Kathmandu
Kolkata Mumbai

Copyright © Shruti Johri 2017

This is a work of fiction. Names, characters, places and incidents are either
the product of the author's imagination or are used fictitiously and any
resemblance to any actual person, living or dead, events or
locales is entirely coincidental.

All rights reserved.

No part of this publication may be reproduced, transmitted,
or stored in a retrieval system, in any form or by any means,
electronic, mechanical, photocopying, recording or otherwise,
without the prior permission of the publisher.

ISBN: 978-81-291-xxxx-x

First impression 2017

10 9 8 7 6 5 4 3 2 1

The moral right of the author has been asserted.

Printed in India by xxxx

This book is sold subject to the condition that it shall not,
by way of trade or otherwise, be lent, resold, hired out, or otherwise
circulated, without the publisher's prior consent, in any form of binding or
cover other than that in which it is published.

To the loving memory of my mother
For the selfless spirit of hospitality

CONTENTS

From the Author ix

THE 'NAÏVE LEARNER'...

Wasted Testimony	3
Tender Bartender	12
The Carnal Getaway	45

... WHO BECAME A 'REBEL EXECUTIVE'

Diplo-Mazey!	71
Face of a Mob	92

... THEN, A 'MELLOWED MANAGER'

Did Eye Lie?	115
Lost and Found	133
The Checkout	151

A NEW CHECK-IN!

Acknowledgements 171

FROM THE AUTHOR

She opens rooms over a million times, day and night, year after year. Vacant rooms, occupied rooms, dirty rooms. Sea-facing rooms, tomb-facing rooms, pool-facing rooms, golf course-facing rooms and the humble city-facing rooms. VIP rooms, budget rooms, honeymoon rooms, delegation rooms, crew rooms, rooms for the handicapped. Twin-bed rooms, double-bed rooms, extra-bed rooms, suites—all with visuals and experiences unheard of!

She is Gauri, a housekeeper at a leading five-star hotel in India.

The minute she steps into a room, a different world opens up in front of her! Each room speaks to her about the nature of its occupant—religious, because an incense stick burns at some corner; upscale, since the room gives away the fragrance of expensive perfumes and deodorants; gluttonous, as she spots crowded cigarette butts in the ashtray along with a dinner tray full of chewed-up bones and empty minibar bottles.

Carnal visuals in the room reveal events that might have taken place. Used condoms thrown carelessly into the toilet, in the dustbin or over the vanity counter. Sticky sex toys and accessories strewn all over the floor and on the bed, blood-stained sheets after young girls hurriedly vacate the rooms early morning.

Innumerable stories lie behind the 'Do Not Disturb' door cards—stories about their occupants, episodes of infidelity, bigotry, absurdity and, most valuable of all, about assorted human behaviour. Flashy German cars, American gadgets and French accessories, but also, the lonely look on the faces of long-staying guests, the homesick expressions of corporate travellers—the symbols of success, prosperity and happiness on one side, and of neglect, abuse and isolation on the other.

Gauri spots customers seeking warmth and meaning from the hotel staff. She sees guests in deep conversations with the bartenders, housekeepers, page boys and guest relations executives. These are simple interactions to unearth backstage scenes, wondering what lies behind the closed service doors and where the staff members dress up in such elaborate uniforms. Thoughtful customers are also concerned if the benefits of working in the hotel match up to the gruelling work hours.

She can feel it in the voices of the hotel guests at the housekeeping desk phone. Their need for love and attention is masked in petty complaints and demands for extra towels, soaps and moisturizers. And their desire for social involvement is conveyed through special requests for holiday-activity planning, personalized food menu or extra flowers.

Despite such intense human involvement as part of their daily work, the life of hoteliers in India is shrouded with stereotypes. Also, their 'services' are often confused with 'servitude'. Does working in hotels only mean cooking and serving, making beds and cleaning toilets?

Time and again, Gauri's illustrious middle class family of scientists, academicians and musicians have been curious to know what work she does in a hotel. They often question her decision to pursue this career, so ordinary by their standards. Close friends and schoolmates from her sleepy hometown ask if 'Housekeeping' is indeed a serious profession. They wonder is it safe for respectable women to work in this industry. They sympathize with her for not being able to make it in engineering, medicine, banking, strategy consulting or law.

This book captures the dilemmas that haunt Gauri during the long hours of work commute on local trains and taxis. Inescapable introspection! She harbours a deep desire to know if her job even matters to anyone. She spots instances when the 'housekeeper' rises above situations and creates a difference in the lives of people around her.

For example, she comforts a widowed businessman who believes that the painting in his hotel room is haunted by a ghost. The mystery finally gets solved in 'Did Eye Lie?'

In 'Tender Bartender', she provides comfort to an ageing Kashmiri barkeeper with her youthful company as he shares his stories of bereavement, of losing his family to militancy and an unrequited love. The barkeeper leaves Gauri with a secret that she must guard to save one of the biggest business empires.

Gauri, when pregnant with her first child, goes out of her way to help a young executive whose job is at stake for losing a CD. 'Lost and Found' traces the search operation that churns out a continuum of strangers helping each other.

Sadly, she also comes face-to-face with missed opportunities when she chooses to adhere to protocol and remain a mute spectator.

She is unable to save a young Bihari migrant from losing his window-cleaning job at the hotel in 'The Wasted Testimony'.

Closet voyeurs, familiar with Gauri, wish to partake in the sleazy stories fanned within the privacy of a hotel room. But she has witnessed extreme eroticism turn into a dangerous obsession. In 'The Carnal Getaway', she recounts horrifying experiences of sex workers at the hands of a perverted politician and a ruthless Arab sheikh.

And then, there are some behind-the-scenes candid moments that travellers always want to know.

Gauri struggles to preserve her sanity at the Indian state-sponsored events in 'Diplo-Mazey'. A snooty protocol officer and his sycophants have no regard for the hard-work done by the hotel staff. Never mind! A humble crow brings divine justice for all, finally.

She highlights the comedy of errors resulting from daily encounters of an English-ignorant houseman in 'Face of a Mob'. These errors lead the reader to the pink panties of a middle-aged corporate English woman.

The book ends with Gauri's interview when she knits all the stories together. She realizes that each story is bound to another through fate or action.

Behind these accounts lies the subtle story of her evolution; of how Gauri gets exploited for her small-town innocence and middle class virtues. Then, dissent rises against the system and she arms herself with the new-found learning of some tricks of the trade. But her empathy melts the bitterness away in favour of the higher levels of experience. She enjoys simple human interactions more than outwitting guests and surpassing bosses and colleagues. Yet some constant work conflicts and personal upheavals re-shape her priorities and Gauri quits hotels.

While written accounts of well-regarded ex-armymen, entrepreneurs, politicians, scientists, travellers, media professionals and social workers dominate the native bookshelves, hospitality stays a lesser-known profession.

Much has been written, read and talked about star hotels in the western world, whereas tales from India still remain untold.

It's time we read these stories!

THE 'NAÏVE LEARNER'...

Meet Gauri.

Barely out of college, she enters the world of hotels as a management trainee. She explores the streets of Jaipur and local trains in Mumbai. She feels overwhelmed with the challenges of an independent life in the metro cities. Her tender age and slender body do little to mask her small-town innocence. Her efforts to please everyone at work are suggestive of certain service-oriented values inherited from the great Indian middle class.

She undergoes intense training at the shop floor level—cleaning toilets, making beds, arranging flowers and laundry operations. It is coupled with the more rational learning of preparing budgets, placing orders, operating the intranet and internet, giving presentations and manpower planning among other skills.

Now, she tells her stories!

WASTED TESTIMONY

The hotel was a melting pot of cultures and vultures!

It was the perfect destination for scores of men and women, not just for business or pleasure but even for employment, as it offered positions ranging from white-collared executives, to blue-collared supervisors, to brown-collared workers, to no-collared labourers.

While it was a culture shock for educated youth from smaller towns, who joined the hotel as supervisors and executives, the labourers and entry-level staff viewed it as an entirely new civilization. These men had left their villages and moved to the cities due to extreme poverty. Some wives joined their men, but most of them stayed behind, nurturing children, labouring on farms, taking care of old parents and awaiting their husbands' occasional return to give them momentary relief, and at times, even deadly venereal diseases.

Mostly naïve, these young migrants were given temporary contract-based employment as plumbers, cooks, painters, polishers, masons, electricians, dishwashers, stewards and window cleaners. Absence of identity proofs and their sudden unexplained disappearances dissuaded the hotel management from giving them permanent employment. Politically and racially motivated, trade unions always tried to cast them into their own moulds. Helpless and powerless, they usually herded together and lived in ghettos to shield themselves from the hideousness of urban life.

As I had also left home at a young age to work and make a career for myself, I shared a special bond with them. I was their formal job trainer and also an informal counsellor. Our afternoon training sessions would often end in personal counselling where I tried to find answers to their real and rational questions.

'Gauri ma'am, how do I send money to my family?'

'Can I call home from the hotel phone? I need to speak urgently with my cousin. His father committed suicide because of failed crops and an unpaid loan.'

'I think I am terribly sick. Which hospital should I visit? Can you lend me some money for the treatment?'

'The police forced our landlord to throw us out of the rented room as our identification papers were not complete. We all had been living together in the shared accommodation. Can you help us find a room again?'

'Bhola, the son of the secretary of the workers' union, had lent me money last month. He is demanding it back at a very high interest rate. What can I do?'

It was rare for me to find well-suited answers. I could only offer them a shoulder to cry on in times of distress, cake and sweets during birthdays and festivals, or contact details of social welfare organizations, but nothing more.

One incident still stands out clearly in my mind. It was barely my second year at work. I was still learning and trying to find a voice of my own among the well-respected and influential seniors.

◆

'I have been waiting here for too long! Can I have the room numbers, Gauri ma'am?'

I lifted my gaze from the duty register to look at the source of this impatient voice that was adding to the chaos around me. It was Chotu, the window cleaner.

Chotu, a young lad from rural Bihar, always maintained a stoic silence throughout duty hours. He wasn't really popular among the local hotel staff who often mistook his quietude for condescension. But that didn't bother him much, since he was staying with his village kinsmen who fulfilled his need for affection and company.

He also exhibited a great deal of sincerity towards his work. And everyone felt amused with his funny style of walking along with the cleaning gear secured tightly around his waist and shoulders at all times. Nothing could separate him from those belts and chains! Be it in the staff cafeteria or the staff lockers, you could always see him strapped and ready. He also carried a small bucket with dusters and tiny squeegees peeping out of it. He looked more like a tortoise carrying its shell.

Nevertheless, I found him endearing. I could barely hold the slightest of wrath against his quiet disposition housed within a small frame, giving out a naïve gaze, full of honesty... And, he knew it!

Early mornings can be extremely noisy and confusing for housekeeping. The task of allocating huge volume of duties to a staff of modest number is often made worse with the last minute truancy of team members. Then, there is also the challenge of herding the night-duty staff together and requesting them to do a double duty. And, not to forget, the endless guest requests for soaps, ironing, shoe-shines, and extra towels—all streaming in over the phone.

To add to that, the cramped quarters of the housekeeping department are enough to disorient the sanest of minds. There are huge key holders fixed on the walls that store hundreds of keys for cloak rooms, stores, linen chutes, garbage rooms, staff toilets and, of course, the master keys to enter the guest rooms. The pagers and walkie-talkies keep beeping endlessly, only adding to the confusion. Big piles of log books, duty allocation registers, records of leaves, lost and found items, purchase order books and registers crowd the work stations. Defunct vacuum cleaners and floor polishing machines, awaiting repair or exchange, keep blocking the doorways and passages. Obsolete computers and printers that have been discarded from the front line—more glamorous counters like guest relations, reception, concierge and general manager's office—find their way into the humble housekeeping cell, which is often located in the basement, away from the prying eyes of the guests.

And above all, it's customary to have large bright wooden framed pictures with motivational quotes, printed in big and bold letters—T.E.A.M.: Together Everyone Achieves More; Think Outside the Box; Don't Deliver a Product. Deliver an Experience; Recognition is Earned, Never Awarded; It's the Will, not the Skill. These quotes are meant to inspire while you perpetually perspire!

In the hurly-burly of activities, I had completely missed seeing Chotu standing in one corner of the room, waiting for his daily list of rooms in need of window cleaning.

'You don't have to be so anxious, do you?' I said while handing him a small scroll of paper with room numbers scribbled on it.

'All the windows on the fifth floor have to be cleaned properly from outside. Those rooms that are under repair will be released tomorrow. Got it, Chotu?' I asked.

Chotu, being true to his nature, did not reply and left hurriedly towards the service elevators. He was going to have a long day, after all!

◆

A few hours later, I got a series of frantic messages on my pager from Vasudha, the desk operator.

For the uninitiated, pager was one of the hottest status symbols of the mid-nineties. Sadly, it was slowly strangled to death by its elder brother—the mobile phone, over the next decade or so. However, during those days, even the CEOs used to carry one, flaunting the 'anytime-anywhere' beep from below their belts. The female hotel staff, on the other hand, fastened the pager at their waist, over their uniform saris.

So, as soon as I read the messages from Vasudha, I darted to the nearest telephone and called her.

'Ma'am, come downstairs quickly to the housekeeping department,' she said, 'It is about Chotu!'

I rushed to the department with fearful thoughts flitting through my mind. I hoped against hope that no accident had occurred. Did Chotu's belt snap while he was cleaning? Or did he slip off the building? I felt my mind race ahead of my feet as I opened the door.

There he stood, devoid of his shell for the first time! His cleaning gear was packed and placed neatly behind him on the floor. He had been summoned by the Human Resources department and I had been given the charge to follow through.

'What's the matter, Chotu?' I asked, concerned.

'Let us reach the HR office, ma'am. You will find out everything,' he replied in a dejected tone.

◆

'Mr Kaushik has been waiting for you, ma'am. Please meet him in his office quickly.'

I was ushered into the manager's office with these words

by Anita, his personal assistant. I pulled Chotu along with me, holding his hands.

Mr Kaushik's office seemed different today. Instead of the bustling activity that one associated with a regular week day, the department was deserted. It looked as if the staff had been sent away, maybe deliberately, to the canteen or for their smoke breaks. There was a deathly silence all around as he sat on his chair looking like a distressed judge about to award life sentence to a convict during a courtroom trial. He turned some papers over hurriedly and indicated to us to be seated, flashing a pseudo-courteous smile.

Mr Arvind Kaushik was feared and hated most among the hotel staff. He derived his power from one single talent—keeping the general manager and the union leaders appeased and flattered at all times. Although in his mid-forties, he seemed to have aged much ahead of his peers.

'Okay, Chotu. Can you tell us what happened?' asked Mr Kaushik, clearing his throat.

'Why do you ask, sir? You know about the incident, don't you? I feel awkward talking about it in front of Gauri ma'am,' replied Chotu tilting his head towards me.

'That's so impressive, Chotu. How I wish this sense of discretion had prevailed earlier? Now, speak!'

After a few seconds of silence, Chotu continued, 'I was cleaning the windows of the rooms under repair on the fifth floor. Those windows were very dirty and it took me longer than usual to clean each one of them. Gauri ma'am had informed me that none of the fifth floor rooms had guests staying in them. So, I started cleaning the windows by moving along the outside ledge as it would be faster than entering through the rooms. I started my work at Room 501 and reached Room 517. But I had barely started cleaning the windows of

Room 517 when…' Chotu paused nervously, biting his lips, unable to lift his eyes.

'Please continue, Chotu. Tell us exactly what happened!' demanded Mr Kaushik.

'I had begun cleaning the windows when I saw GM sir inside that room,' Chotu said.

'Okay. So you saw our General Manager Mr Dhir inside the room. What about him?' I questioned Chotu.

'GM sir was inside the room…along with that tall ma'am from the office that is next to us.'

'You mean Shalini ma'am from Sales and Marketing?' I asked in disbelief.

'Yes ma'am. They were together in bed!' Chotu's eyes suddenly lit up. I was shocked to witness the ever-silent Chotu turn into a garrulous kid, charting out the incident in detail.

He took a deep breath and continued, 'It was some sight! Shalini ma'am is so beautiful. I could not take my eyes off her as she lay on the bed. I noticed GM sir much later. He was squatting beside her…'

'Chotu!' I shouted out his name to awaken him from his daydream.

Meanwhile, Mr Kaushik gave me a scornful look which reminded me of a kindergarten child whose ice cream had been snatched away by bullies!

'Ma'am,' he continued, 'I am a twenty-one year old boy staying away from my poor family for the last eight years. I started working as a child, washing plates at roadside eateries before picking up this respectable job three years back. Every month, I send my entire salary to my family. Seeing something like this was new to me and I could not help myself from getting carried away. And this is the truth. What have I done wrong? I have been asked to discontinue my services in the hotel with immediate effect. Why am I being punished?'

'I am sorry to say that you have let all of us down, Chotu,' Mr Kaushik intervened.

'None of the hotel employees have ever behaved in such an atrocious fashion. You have no regard for the seniors in this hotel, if I may say so. Please sign this letter and contact the Accounts department regarding your full and final clearance.'

'If that is the case, I am really sorry, sir. I apologize for the disrespect I might have shown towards my seniors,' he said, signing the letter.

'You need to sign here as a management witness,' Mr Kaushik said to me. I signed mutely as I glanced through the last paragraph of the document which stated that sexual abuse towards co-employees was the reason for termination of Chotu's services. It was addressed to the outsourced agency.

Mr Kaushik called the GM's office immediately to update his boss about the dismissal of the 'ill-mannered' window cleaner.

Chotu left the office without remorse. He spoke about the incident with every single person he met in the staff basement corridor. I followed him slowly. How I wished to offer him help and some consolation. But apparently, he did not need anything. Perhaps he knew he would get another job—he knew it too well! In a city dotted with high-rise buildings, there was no dearth of jobs for a window cleaner. In fact, hardworking and fearless workers like him, who were ready to brave the weather and the heights to ensure sparkling windows for an enticing view were always in demand.

I could not walk any further. I stood in front of the staff notice board pretending to read it. I could hear Chotu's steps and voice fade away as he went farther into the corridor and talked to someone familiar.

He was asked, 'Chotu, we are feeling very bad for you. Are you okay?'

He replied, 'I have never felt better! It was such a divine sight. All I ask from God is one experience like that in heaven and in return, I am ready to live the rest of my life in hell!'

After Chotu's voice had vanished away with him, I walked back to my department at a slow pace.

'Reception wants the fifth floor rooms to be cleared, ma'am. What do I tell them?' Vasudha reminded me of the pending work while putting a call on hold.

'Tell them that the room windows are dirty because there is only one window cleaner today for all the guest rooms on the fifth floor,' I replied, irritably. 'The work will be completed only by late evening and that's when the rooms can be handed over for occupancy.'

'Reception says that the guests don't care about the view at night,' Vasudha passed on the message in an indifferent manner and added, 'and we can clean the remaining windows tomorrow morning.'

Feeling annoyed with the apathy for window cleaning, I rushed and snatched the phone away from Vasudha, 'So, according to you, guests don't care about clean windows? Do you even know what it takes to clean the windows? Can you imagine what it must feel like to be suspended multiple floors above the ground, where the only thing between you and a possible death is the waist belt?'

There was a short spell of silence over the phone.

I could feel a lump forming in my throat as I tried to justify my unexpected outburst to the reception staff. Just then my eyes fell on one of the motivational quotes displayed on the wall behind the desk—

'THE SHOW MUST GO ON'.

TENDER BARTENDER

'Do you feel fine, Shekhar?' I asked with concern.

He sat hidden in the staff parking lot, on the cement pavement behind his antique van. He seemed to be in no hurry to reach home, despite having completed his shift. Deep in thought, he sat resting his head over his palms, a pile of cigarette stubs lying beside him. There was a lingering odour of smoke around him.

'How long have you been sitting here, Shekhar? And didn't the security guard stop you from smoking in the parking lot?'

Since there was no reaction from him, I walked closer to take a better look at him. I sat down beside him and took a deep breath. A long silence followed.

Shekhar Wakhloo was one of the oldest and finest bartenders in town, almost like a long-cherished trophy of the hotel. He was part of the exodus of Kashmiri pandits that began in the mid '80s and had found his new home here. Having lost most of his immediate family, he had made a humble start for himself by taking up a hotel job as a steward. It was a rather unusual choice for a well-read person with a sound academic background, more so, considering Shekhar's rich ethnicity. Nevertheless, thanks to his diligence and wit, he quickly rose to the ranks of supervisory positions in restaurants and banquets.

But later on, he began displaying an apathetic attitude towards promotion offers that were made to him regarding executive roles. Despite being hounded and pursued by the senior management for years, he chose to settle down as the chief bartender at the lounge bar for the larger and final part of his career. Although he was a teetotaller himself, Shekhar won innumerable accolades for the hotel at various bartending and cocktail-making championships. Even at fifty, he alternated between creativity and managing resources with such ease that it made him indispensable to the hotel. While the hotel did have a manager at the bar, that position was rendered ornamental due to the dexterity and aura of Shekhar—the real power centre of the bar!

There was a mysterious attraction about him. He was a bachelor and reasonably good-looking, although he had just a few years left before retirement. One could ponder—why did he refuse those promotions and salary raises? Why was he still unmarried? Did he ever fall in love?

But Shekhar remained reticent. He seemed unmindful to all the whispers and gossip around him. Strong as the wall of a fort, he never let his guard down at work, although he did enjoy a close-knit circle of friends. It was also widely known that his chosen pals meant nothing short of a family to him. Be it good times or bad, Shekhar stood by them like a pillar of strength.

Sitting beside him on the pavement, I was still waiting for him to talk to me. Right then, it felt a little bizarre to encounter him in one of his unguarded moments. I held his left hand and bent my head to catch his eye as he sat there, slumped.

Finally, Shekhar responded with a faint smile and asked, 'Can we talk for a while?'

I glanced at my wristwatch and said, 'Shekhar, I hope you are not sick? I thought you were feeling somewhat weak. And, aren't these too many cigarettes at one go? Actually, I...'

'I am perfectly healthy. You don't have to stay if you have something else to attend to. It's fine with me. And don't you worry about me! Please carry on.'

I wasn't sure if it was genuine concern and empathy for Shekhar, or just plain curiosity, but I decided to stay with him for a while. After all, my social standing as a single young executive fresh-out-of-college couldn't be easily threatened or inconvenienced by spending an evening with this elderly bartender. The synergy Shekhar and I shared had been evident during the renovation of the lounge bar, when we had worked well in tandem. Perhaps, he wished to extend our professional comfort into a more personal space.

And, truth be told, I felt privileged to be one of the chosen ones, given his fussy selection of close companions at work!

'Oh, that's okay, Shekhar. I am free. But let's sit somewhere more comfortable.'

'Sure. Shall we sit over there?' Shekhar replied pointing to a wooden bench a little away from the parking area. Although rickety, it did offer undisturbed private space.

I nodded in agreement and replied with a grin, 'Only if you promise not to smoke any more cigarettes while we talk.'

He consented and we got up to go and occupy the bench. Shekhar was dressed casually in a comfortable pair of grey jeans and white t-shirt. He had a fairly robust body for a man of his age, with reasonably toned muscles, even around the waist and shoulders. He had close cropped grey hair around a clean-shaven face, and had a well-defined jawline. After all, his job required him to remain youthful and well-groomed at all times.

'You look so different out of the uniform sari,' Shekhar remarked about my appearance. I caught him glancing at me from the corner of his eyes. I was wearing a half-sleeved striped midi dress over a pair of strappy sandals.

'Well, different as in nice or different as in odd?' I smiled.

'Nice. Very nice,' he clarified.

After another short spell of silence, Shekhar resumed talking again.

'Are you interested in sculptures? Clay sculptures, in particular?'

I felt that the conversation had taken a strange turn. Was it bait for a date? Why were we discussing my attire and hobbies? Nevertheless, I played along.

'Nah!' I replied with a slight shrug.

'So, you might not have visited the clay sculpture exhibition at our ballroom.'

'Oh that! I did go for an inspection of the ballroom in the morning today. There was a complaint that there were coffee stains on the banquet hall carpet. The carpet crew had a tough time removing the blotch.'

'What else did you see?'

'Well, I also chanced upon the display of life-sized clay models on sculpture stands. They were mostly human figures, busts and torsos, in greyish-brown. I really didn't notice anything more than that,' I thought for a while before adding, 'Yeah, that's pretty much it!'

'Hmm,' Shekhar took a deep breath before continuing, 'Let me tell you the true story of a sculptor who visited our hotel almost fifteen years ago. It was during that time that I developed a keen interest in clay sculptures.'

There was a sudden flush of joy on Shekhar's face as he began narrating the account. His eyes lit up with delight and a soft smile touched his lips.

♦

Shekhar began the story...

It was quite late at night. With hardly half an hour left for the bar to close, I hurriedly took the last drink orders. Just then, the door was thrown open by a young woman who made a rather brash entry into the bar. She headed straight to the counter and perched herself upon one of the bar stools. She kept fiddling with the hem of her dress before summoning one of the junior stewards with a rude gesture of her finger. From a distance, it seemed as if she was in disagreement with the steward over something. Sensing danger, I rushed to the counter to attend to her.

'Good evening, ma'am. Welcome to the lounge bar! What can I serve you?'

'Vodka with tonic water and make it large. Serve me at least four glasses, all at once,' she replied hurriedly and then pointed at the junior steward, 'Your friend, over there, seems to be upset about my late arrival. I had barely entered and he ordered me to clear out from the bar in the next half an hour. Curse you all! Why close a bar this early? Are you fond of harassing the hotel residents?'

It was pointless to explain the bar permit and liquor license matters to her since she seemed too angry to be reasoned with. Instead, I simply said, 'Sure, ma'am. Your drinks will be served shortly. Just to clarify once more, did you just order four large vodkas to drink here?' Then, I added carefully, 'I mean, there is just half an hour left for the bar...'

I had barely finished before she interrupted again, 'Mister! Are you trying to tell me how much I should drink? Why? Is it because I am a woman who chose to come here alone? You male chauvinist rascals are such poor salesmen! Serve the drinks right away and bill it to Suite 1020.'

I quickly laid four glasses of drinks over the bar counter.

Although busy with bar-closing activities, I kept a watchful eye on her as she drank quickly. She seemed young, and was largely unkempt with untidy hair with no trace of any make-up. She had thrown a crumpled shawl over an old-fashioned dress. But it were her hands that drew my attention. She had hard-working hands! As she held the glass, I could see her dry hands with bulging veins all over them. The nails had been filed down as much as was possible and the skin around them was peeling off. It was rare to spot a woman dressed so carelessly at the hotel. More often than not, ladies would frequent the bar in the best of attires, seductively made-up in rich cosmetics and perfumes.

What if she was an imposter in search of free drinks? I quickly called up the reception to find out who was staying in Suite 1020. The receptionist informed me that the suite was assigned to one Mr Trigunesh Kumar, Managing Director of a large business conglomerate called Shoolin Industries. Mr Kumar had checked into the hotel almost a week back along with his wife, Mrs Bhumija Kumar. The guest couple enjoyed a VVIP status at the hotel and were expected to stay for at least eight months.

The receptionist also alerted me about Mrs Kumar being exceptionally eccentric. The housekeeping staff and the butler who had attended to her in the suite described her as withdrawn. She seemed to have no regard for the opulent hotel or towards the hotel staff who were pampering her endlessly. She also did not seem to care much about her esteemed status of being the wife of a powerful industrial icon. She didn't care about her appearance and chose to wear simple clothes while the expensive ones peeked out from inside her huge half-open trunks that were stacked, rather carelessly, in one corner of the suite. But nothing irked her more than being disturbed by the hotel staff. Everyone, from room cleaning, to laundry pickup to food orders, had to comply with her timings. She preferred the privacy of her suite and that is why when I called the receptionist, she reacted a bit surprised about her late night visit to the bar. I was cautioned to handle her with extreme care, as Shoolin Industries gave a lot of business to the hotel through its room bookings and conferences.

I disconnected the phone and approached the guest with fresh caution and care. By now, she had emptied all the four glasses. It was easy to notice her inebriated state. Her body almost slumped over the bar counter as she struggled to sit upright. With her eyes out of focus, she demanded more drinks in slurred speech. The bar had closed down by then. I politely refused her more drinks, speaking with great reluctance, 'Mrs Kumar, I regret to inform you that the bar is closed. Kindly accept my sincere apologies. Would you like any assistance in going back to your suite?'

'Curse you all, curse you...'

The spiteful words had barely come out of her mouth when she slipped off the bar stool and landed on her knees. Unable to cope with the heavy dose of alcohol, her body convulsed to throw up. I watched on helplessly as she gagged and choked on the carpet, unaware of her surroundings. The staff at the lounge bar exchanged some meaningful yet mischievous glances with each other, as she fell on her stomach on the carpet.

After the violent bout of vomiting, Mrs Kumar was about to collapse, with her face on the floor, when I rushed to pick her up. She had soiled her face and clothes, and looked miserable. After placing her on a three-seater sofa in the restaurant, I rushed out to fetch the security and female staff along with a wheelchair from the bell desk.

'Call Dr Nigam for 1020,' I told the receptionist while

rushing Mrs Kumar back to her room on the hotel wheelchair. We were accompanied by the security guard and a female housekeeper. I felt a little sorry for her pitiable state as she continued to moan painfully.

We found the suite empty. Perhaps Mr Kumar was travelling. Nevertheless, we could not have left her, all sick and alone in the room. The housekeeper cleaned and changed Mrs Kumar in the bathroom while we stood right outside. After putting Mrs Kumar on the four-poster king-size bed, we waited for Dr Nigam in the living area.

Amid the royal opulence of the suite, one mysterious corner lay hidden behind huge wooden partitions. It was dimly lit and its wooden floor was covered with discarded linen. I peeped in curiously to see what lay on the other side.

It was a different world altogether!

Life-sized human clay models, some finished and others not, had been placed carefully over wooden blocks and modelling stands. To my amateur eyes, the works of art appeared to be nothing short of masterpieces. The intricate detailing of the human torsos and busts in clay was stupendous. A central workstation had been set up beside the large modelling stand. Huge packets of modelling clay were stacked in one corner. It was interesting to see various sculpting tools laid out meticulously. Callipers, palettes and scrapers, spatulas, cutters, knives, loose wires, wire gauze, scalpels, broom brushes, sand papers and a wearable magnifying glass adorned the worktable. An adjustable sculpting stool for the artist had also been set beside the worktable.

One could clearly see the milestones in the artistic journey while looking at those clay models. They included half-finished armatures in aluminium wire frames, raw structures in oil clay and many works in progress.

I could sense a distinct energy in the makeshift clay sculpting studio.

'Step away from there!' the housekeeper hissed, panicking. She added, 'Mrs Kumar gets very angry if anybody from the hotel enters this part of her suite.'

I immediately stepped away from the sculpting corner and joined my colleagues in their wait for Dr Nigam. Soon enough, the doctor arrived and examined Mrs Kumar as she lay still on her bed. The doctor assured us that the lady was fine and in deep sleep. Her body had already thrown out the excess alcohol and there wasn't much to worry about. She was expected to recover completely by morning. Dr Nigam also advised serving some strong coffee and aspirin when she gets up, but only with Mrs Kumar's approval.

A formal note was written for Mrs Kumar and left at the bedside table. It informed her of her sudden bout of illness at the lounge bar and the subsequent visit made by Dr Nigam. Thereafter, we all left the suite and carried on with our usual business.

The next morning, just as I entered the lounge bar, the phone rang. It was the telephone operator.

'Hi! Mrs Bhumija Kumar from Suite 1020 wishes to speak with you. Shall I connect you to her room!'

I was taken aback a little. Nevertheless, I had to comply with the request of a resident guest.

'Sure. Please connect the phone.'

'Hello,' said Mrs Kumar in a deep voice.

'Good morning, Mrs Kumar! This is Shekhar from the lounge bar. I hope you had a good night's rest!'

'Yes. I wish to thank all the hotel staff who helped me up to my room. Is the bar open?'

'The bar will reopen in the next half an hour, ma'am. We

look forward to welcoming you...'

'Where are the other staff members from last night?'

'Don't worry, Mrs Kumar, I shall have them meet you in your room.'

'Thanks.'

After informing the female housekeeper and security guard of Mrs Kumar's desire to meet them, I continued with my work as usual. The beverage inventory was done; glassware, cutlery and crockery cleaned, stacked and arranged; table cloth and napkins set; lemon wedges and other garnishes chopped. Housekeeping was also done with the carpet and furniture cleaning and the florist brought in lovely rose bowl arrangements for the tables.

The bar opened as usual at eleven in the morning. For the most part, afternoons at the bar are quiet with very few guests walking in, whereas evenings and weekends get quite frantic!

I was adjusting newspapers and magazines over the reading stand when Mrs Bhumija Kumar came into the bar.

A little unsure, she stepped inside carefully. She was looking for something intently. I stole a moment to admire her calm and composed disposition, a far cry from the unruly act she had put up the night before. The informal sense of dressing, however, had not changed. The formal dressing code at the lounge bar could be damned! No one dared to question and risk displeasing the heiress of Shoolin Industries and wife of Mr Trigunesh Kumar. I couldn't help but notice the hotel towelling slippers that she wore. Freshly bathed and dressed in plain white linen shirt and pyjamas, she pulled her wet hair forward. A small patch of skin on her back was visible under the wet shirt.

Without startling her, I moved slowly into her line of sight. Then, I cleared my throat and said, 'Good morning, Mrs

Kumar! Welcome to the lounge bar. I hope you feel fine now?'

Mrs Kumar turned around and smiled, 'Yes, I took some coffee and aspirin. And thank you for taking such good care of me last night,' she said and slipped her hands quickly into her pockets and took out a bundle of notes.

She held the money out in front of me and continued, 'Please accept this as a small token of my appreciation.'

'Oh! This is so kind of you, ma'am but this won't be necessary at all. It was part of my duty to take care of you.'

After a few more unsuccessful attempts at tipping me, Mrs Kumar expressed her wish to buy some drinks at the bar counter. I could sense the despair in her voice to compensate for last night's misbehaviour.

'I need to drink something wholesome. How about a fruit juice cocktail? Without any spirit?' she said after occupying one of the bar stools.

'That's a good choice, ma'am. It shall be served to you right away.'

'How long have you worked here, Shekhar?' asked Mrs Kumar, after she had read my name on the uniform tag.

'A little over a year now,' I replied, handing over the fruit juice cocktail in a tall glass.

As she drank, her eyes were focused on me. Oh, how I loved the attention! Not that it was my first instance of being in the spotlight. As a bartender, I had to entertain lonely guests, mostly men, by striking conversations about sports, politics, social trends and 'women'. A few drinks down, some of them even confided their deep dark secrets. There had been times when the hotel bar seemed to resemble a church confession room. But, now, here was a woman sitting alone at the bar, who was none other than Mrs Bhumija Kumar. This is going to be an interesting weekday morning at the bar, I thought to myself.

I straightened my waistcoat, readjusted the shirt cuffs and pulled my shoulders back after drawing in a deep breath. We were alone at the bar. It was important for me to appear occupied with work, lest she started feeling awkward and withdrew her gaze. So, my hands ran over tasks which had already been completed. I began inspecting the cigar box, adjusting the beer dispenser and the spirit bottles and made a few unnecessary follow-up calls here and there. And, all this while, her gaze followed my every move, just what I discreetly desired. The description of Mrs Kumar provided by the receptionist had fuelled my curiosity to know more about her. Why was she withdrawn? What made her so indifferent towards the riches and comforts that surrounded her? Was she in an unhappy marriage with Trigunesh Kumar? What did she do in the privacy of her big suite, all alone? She was a puzzle, waiting to be solved. What more could I have asked for on that idle morning at the bar?

'You know, the security guard and the housekeeper accepted the tip so gracefully,' Mrs Kumar mumbled.

'Ma'am, you are too generous. But it really won't be necessary,' I replied.

'What's your full name? Where are you from?' she asked.

'Shekhar Wakhloo. I am from Kashmir, ma'am.'

'You stay with your family here?'

'No, ma'am, I stay alone. My family is no more. But I do visit a couple of distant relatives who live in this city, occasionally.'

'Oh! I am so sorry.'

There was a respectful silence. But, for the first time, talking about my deceased family didn't hurt as much as it did usually. The excitement of being able to spend a quiet morning alone with a female member of the elite society was exhilarating. It felt great to strike a meaningful conversation with a lady.

Soon, we started talking casually on a variety of subjects, ranging from hangover remedies to newspaper headlines.

I noticed several different things about her. To begin with, she wasn't the regular trophy wife of a rich industrialist; not once did her background matter during our chat. She loved to talk and interact with me, somewhat in sharp contrast to her description given by the receptionist the previous night. I secretly knew she was an artist and artists are moody! Thus, it became easy for me to understand her sudden bouts of silence and withdrawal. I also found her quite pretty. Yes, she had a very lively face beneath all that outer shabbiness.

'One more, please!' Mrs Kumar requested another glass of fruit cocktail.

'Just like last night, ma'am?' I asked rather audaciously.

After a brief pause, she burst out laughing uncontrollably. I chuckled along with her, pleased that she had begun to warm up to me.

And then she asked me, 'What do you like most about your work?'

With a small smile on my lips, I began showing off a few bartending tricks. She became engrossed in watching me as I shook and mixed the cocktail shaker before flipping and juggling the glasses. She clapped at the end of each act as I took a deep bow.

Time flew quite fast and we both did not realize when two hours had passed. If it was not for the manager who visited the bar on an inspection round, we would have carried on with our little rendezvous. Mrs Kumar chose to remain aloof to the pleasantries offered by the manager. Instead, she descended from the bar stool and walked towards the door. Now, I definitely felt like the privileged one!

She turned and said, 'Thank you for the lovely drinks,

Shekhar. See you again. And, by the way, you can bill the drinks to my room account.'

I escorted Mrs Kumar to the door and bid her goodbye with a warm smile. A special chord had struck between us. Deep down, I was sure of having more such tête-à-têtes with her.

Sure enough, Mrs Kumar began frequenting the lounge bar, especially in the mornings, given that the evenings brought with them other guests and more staff members who crowded the bar. She visited the bar alone since her husband had important business matters to sort out during the day. We used to talk and debate, and then either reconcile or disagree on a variety of topics. She came across as a well read and informed person. I remember reading the news headlines just before her visits so I could flaunt my knowledge about current affairs. I also scanned book reviews so I could boast to have read the critically-acclaimed ones without having actually read any.

Since I had not been lucky with women even at thirty-five, save a few meaningless flings and sexual encounters, I truly desired to be accepted by a well-regarded and mature woman just to prove myself worthy of being a fine suitor in future. Maybe, that is why, I was so keen to impress her. Her simple words of appreciation and her gaze boosted my self-esteem beyond measure. Soon, she seemed to be in awe of my intellect and enterprising disposition.

Ever since losing my family, I had been extremely lonely. It was a constant challenge to keep my mind distracted from the pain of living without them. My heart still bled with terrible flashes of the killings that had taken place. How I had tried to get away from those mental agonies, but nothing seemed to work, until the interesting company of this lady guest offered me just the respite that I had pined for, for so long!

I had also begun to derive a sense of power and importance with my growing acquaintance with her. After all, the hotel staff had been asked to keep the Kumars from Suite 1020 pleased at all times. Thus, on the work front, it fetched more sales at the bar along with some excellent employee recommendations.

I was getting to know her better. But one thing that had me at my wits' end was her stoic silence in response to my questions about her family. This reticence was a far cry from the engaging tone she displayed while discussing everything else. I knew I had to crack this mystery for the puzzle to be fully solved and finally, I did.

'You won't give up asking about my family, will you, Shekhar?' she said as she countered my question regarding her birthplace and parents, one more time.

'I'm sorry about the repeated questions, ma'am. But I'm not sorry about my care and concern for you. I just want to assure myself that you are doing fine! You're free not to answer it again,' I replied, trying to put up an honest face. Actually, I was just plain curious, nothing more than that.

'But then you will ask me again, won't you? Let me finish this matter, right here, right now!' she continued after a small pause, 'I didn't have a glorious childhood to boast about, you know. My dad used to manage the personal accounts and some private matters of Trigunesh's father. He was one of his very few trusted aides. After losing both my parents in a road accident, I was adopted into the Kumar household when I was barely ten. I owe my entire existence to Trigunesh's father, who is my father-in-law now. He ensured a good education and comfortable life for me. He even got me married to his own son.'

'What a great thing to do! Taking care of a needy and helpless child...' I could hardly complete the sentence before

Mrs Kumar cut me short.

'That hurts, you know! Being labelled as needy and helpless! It was not easy for me to accept a different family while I was still bereaving the loss of my own. Or to handle the gossip among friends and relatives about how I took advantage of the kindness shown by the Kumars and trapped Trigunesh into marrying me so that I could become an heir to the Shoolin business empire. Contrast it with what the Kumars had to sacrifice? Nothing! They merely spent an insignificant fraction of their wealth to raise me, that's all. And the continued applause they receive for adopting me outweighs their efforts. But I do feel bad for Trigunesh, you know. He deserved a better life partner than me—a woman of his stature, who could have appreciated all this wealth and status that I still can't consider as my own. I wonder if this shall ever change,' she paused, staring at her own reflection in the mirrored background of the bar counter.

'Am I ungrateful? Possibly yes. But how do I stop these feelings of alienation from affecting my perception of relationships? You are also living an orphaned life, if not... if not a childhood like me. But you have somehow made it on your own, without getting crushed under the weight of endless favours from someone else,' she resumed after a while, 'Do you know why I visited the bar late that night?'

'No ma'am,' I replied, while feeling bad about raking up her apparently painful past.

'That night, Trigunesh had remarked, "You are lifeless." He said that I lock myself inside the suite, eat whatever is thrown at me, and wear the most disgusting old clothes. He asked me to do something different for once. I believe his exact words were, "Step out of this goddamn place and get a life. Be a Kumar." Yeah, that's what he said,' she sat there, smiling slightly, and then added, 'He wasn't entirely wrong in saying that. But it hurt me enough to do things that I usually don't do, like getting drunk all alone in a crowded bar, for instance.'

'Oh! That's alright, ma'am. Nothing happened that night,' I tried comforting her. I had finally made Mrs Kumar trust me enough that she could freely share the sordid details of her private life. Now I wanted to prove myself worthy of that trust. I stepped out of the bar counter and stood beside her. We faced the bar mirror together.

Pointing at her reflection, I asked her, 'Who do you see there, ma'am?'

'That's me, of course,' she answered.

'True. But I also see a person with great self-pride. She wants to achieve something big on her own and she will not rest until it's done. After that, everything will be alright for her.'

'You make it sound so simple.'

Mrs Kumar left the bar in a contemplative manner.

Phew! That was an intense talk with her, I thought to myself. I was not sure where all of this was headed. Perhaps, the highs of seducing a lady of such social standing outweighed any logical or moral bearing for me.

'Call me Bhumi, will you Shekhar?' Mrs Kumar demanded the next morning at the bar. She was behaving quite differently. She spoke and laughed very little. There was a certain amount of tension whenever our eyes met. The gaze in her eyes was too intense for me to stand without showing any signs of discomfort. I had already begun to fidget. And yet, she continued staring at me obstinately.

Just then, another guest walked in unexpectedly, picked up the newspaper and occupied one of the bar stools beside her. He was an elderly gentleman, maybe of Southeast Asian descent. I acknowledged his presence politely and took his order for drinks.

As I prepared his order, Mrs Bhumija Kumar or Bhumi, watched my every move. Her gaze lingered on my chest and shoulders.

'Can I have a notepad and pen, please?' she suddenly asked.

'Sure, ma'am. Here it is,' I stammered while pushing the scribbling pad and a pen towards her.

She wrote a little note and gave it back to me. I quickly tore off the paper and stuffed it inside my pocket. Mrs Kumar left for her suite.

The elderly gentleman lifted his eyes and looked at me with bewilderment. I cleared my throat and smiled back respectfully at him. A couple of drinks later, he too made an exit from the bar.

In all eagerness, I pulled out the scribbled note from my pocket. It read quite simply, 'Come to my suite after lunch. I have something to show you. See you, Bhumi.'

I had mixed feelings upon reading the note. I was scared and excited, both at the same time. What if Mrs Bhumija Kumar had been smitten with my intensity? What if she threw herself upon me in the privacy of her bedroom? Going by her words of last night, she did not seem to share intimate terms with her husband, after all. What if my seniors at work were to find out everything that was happening? What if Mr Trigunesh Kumar came to know of his wife's brewing intimacy with an ordinary bartender like me? And yet, I felt victorious about my secret little conquest of Mrs Kumar's confidence. Having won over her mind and heart with my wit and care, it was time to acquire her physically and completely. It shall be a rendezvous to cherish for a lifetime, I thought to myself!

Never before had I felt the need to look so presentable.

During my lunch break, I bathed and shaved again and wore a fresh set of uniform. I pushed my clean feet into a new pair of socks and slid them into shiny shoes. I patted on some extra eau de cologne over my cheeks while working out careful answers in my mind. Why wasn't I going home that afternoon? Or, what was I doing on the tenth floor outside suite 1020?

Fully dressed, I landed on the tenth floor guest corridor. There was nobody around as the housekeeping staff was still away for their lunch break. I took long strides and quickly walked up to the door of Suite 1020. My heart was pounding louder than the sound of the doorbell.

'Coming,' Mrs Kumar responded in a sweet voice. I could also hear the sound of her steps over the wooden floor, approaching the door quickly.

'Hi!' she said, a bit breathlessly.

'Good afternoon,' I said awkwardly.

'Please come in,' she said with a big smile on her face, and then continued, 'Thanks for the visit. Please sit down.'

She pointed towards the living room sofa.

'Thanks for the invite, ma'am...Bhumija.' I fumbled.

'You're getting close. Bhumi would sound best, you know?' she laughed, 'Would you like to have something? Should I order food or drinks?'

'Thank you. But I have already eaten lunch. And none of my colleagues know that I am here B-Bh Bhumi.'

'Oh, I see. I'm sorry that you went through so much trouble to come and see me.'

She paused and then simply said, 'So, shall we start?'

'Start what?' I asked nervously.

'Come here.'

Bhumi led me to her makeshift clay sculpting studio inside the suite. Little did she know that I had already seen it during the night she had passed out in the bar. Although four months had gone by, everything was still fresh in my mind. The armatures in aluminium wire frames, raw structures in oil clay, life-size finished clay models placed firmly over wooden blocks, central workstation with neatly arranged sculpting tools and the sculptor's seat.

I could make out that the place was not cleaned regularly since housekeeping wasn't allowed to enter it. There was dust all over the furniture and floor with piles of oil clay packets stored in different corners.

There was also a new addition of a tall wooden stool with a round padded seat. A black sheet had been used as a backdrop. Before I could ask anything, Bhumi pointed towards the stool and asked, 'Could you please sit here for a while?'

'Sure,' I perched myself upon the high stool with my long legs bent uncomfortably.

'Let me be honest with you. I have been meaning to create a clay replica of your figure for quite some time now. But it takes time to create such a model. I hope to have your full support. It might get slightly boring at times just sitting here doing nothing. We can play music or you could watch television?'

'Why me?' I asked surprised and a little disappointed.

'That's because you're the perfect muse who has managed to inspire me with his slightest presence. Yesterday, your parting words at the bar were not taken lightly, Shekhar! Indeed, I must do something big and since sculpting is my passion, I cannot think of doing anything else.'

Suddenly, I was upset at being made to feel like a mere art subject. Is this why she had stared at my chest and shoulders all this while? And here I was thinking that I had won the game of seducing none other than Mrs Bhumija Kumar! Oh!

So stupid and naïve of me! I should have known my position, after all. Although it was difficult for me to admit, yet it was not her mistake. She had never led me into believing anything. It was I who had jumped the gun. And, now, I realized as I sat there, uneasily, that it would not be wise to disappoint a guest of her stature. Whatever it was that had begun between the two of us had to be closed tactfully. And who knows? This could be just the beginning of what I secretly desired with Mrs Bhumija Kumar. All in good time, I thought, harder the labour, sweeter the fruit! I just needed more patience.

Perhaps Bhumi caught a little glimpse of my inner tumult and asked, 'Are you lost somewhere, Shekhar?'

'No, not at all!' I answered calmly.

'Good. I need to take a few measurements. Could you please take off your shirt?'

'What? You want me to take off my shirt?'

'I meant just the shirt, Shekhar. Why do you sound so shocked?'

With great reluctance, I removed my shirt and later, even the vest on Bhumi's request. Amid all the confusion, I tried to console myself by noting that at least my efforts to look presentable hadn't gone to waste! Her 'muse', or whatever she chose to call me, was in his best form.

After noticing a scar on the right side of my chest, just below the collar bone, she enquired, 'How did you get the scar?'

'This is a parting gift I received while fleeing from the valley, a scar left from a dagger wound. I heard the killings turned worse with each year. But for my family, the worst happened right at the start itself. Militants had tried to kill me and my family. Well, I was unlucky to escape alone while my family succumbed. The scar looks quite ugly; don't you think?'

Bhumi stopped for a minute, looked into my eyes and

said, 'Sorry to hear about the hell you have been through. And, no, the scar isn't ugly. Have you heard about *Kintsugi*?'

'No ma'am, I have never heard of it,' I acknowledged.

'Well. *Kintsugi* is an ancient form of Japanese art. The philosophy behind it believes that nothing is ever truly broken. Smashed pottery is repaired by using beautiful seams of gold. Each piece created thus, boasts of its fractures and breaks instead of hiding them. *Kintsugi* often makes the repaired piece even more beautiful than the original, infusing it with new spirit. These little imperfections, like this scar of yours, can breathe immense life into the most ordinary pieces of art, and even human existence.'

I was absorbed in the interesting description of *Kintsugi*. As I sat bare-chested atop the wooden stool, Bhumi wore an apron and took out various measuring instruments. It was interesting to note the manner in which she used the calliper, try the square and measuring tape alternately to take detailed measurements of my body. She scribbled on a notepad extensively. Apart from the length, breadth and height of my head, neck and torso, she also recorded other minute details like the drop of my shoulders, the extent of my collar bones and even the rise of my chest.

I wondered how a woman, who is left alone often by her busy husband and is presumably starved of physical affection, could appear this aloof despite seeing a man's bare body. At least that's what she had hinted on the previous day. Or was I jumping the gun again? But Bhumi didn't show even the slightest stir as her fingers and palms rolled all over my naked chest. Such was her focus in studying my body that she hardly took notice of the rising gooseflesh on my arms and ticklish shivers running down my spine on several occasions.

Almost an hour later, Bhumi asked me to wear my vest

and shirt and wait in the sitting room. She took a deep breath and wiped off the little layer of sweat from her forehead. She went inside to wash her hands.

Offering me some orange juice, she said, 'Thank you so much, Shekhar! You were great today.'

'You're almost welcome,' I replied with a wink.

'Ha-ha! I can see that you were bored, perhaps?'

'Well, a little, maybe.'

'I see. Next time, we shall take care of that.'

'Next time?'

'Yes. You have to come here again.'

'Really? How many more sittings before I get to see myself in clay?'

'At least three more. And each of these sittings could last even up to four hours or more.'

I gave her a look of surprise and asked, 'When should I come next? The sittings will have to be planned well.'

'Yes, I understand. Can the next sitting be scheduled for the coming week, same day?'

'Yeah, sure,' I replied. I had made up my mind to help Bhumi out with the clay sculpture.

I finished drinking the glass of juice. It was a very casual goodbye for both of us as I left the suite.

The next few days during that week were terribly lonely, especially the mornings. Quite understandably, Bhumi had been busy sculpting. Or, was she unwell? I used to worry, thinking about how she stayed all alone in the huge suite. It became a secret habit of mine to check her food and drink orders every day at the cashier. She seemed to eat just fine! Was I missing her? It was hard to figure out and even harder to admit. Earlier, I had felt on top and in control of this little wooing game. But now, I wondered many a time—was it just a game? I waited desperately for the week to end so that we could meet again, even if it was meant strictly for art work.

Finally, the day arrived. I began to wonder if Bhumi had forgotten all about our next meeting. Just then, the lounge bar phone rang and I rushed to pick it up. It was indeed her! She reminded me about the scheduled art sitting as I tried my best to sound businesslike.

Without making too much fuss about my appearance, I met her again in her suite. This time, I felt quite collected because, perhaps, my unreal expectations had been tamed. She was an artist and I was her muse. That was the understanding. Bhumi greeted me, quite casually, as if mere hours and not days had separated us. She looked just fine but was too engrossed in her work.

I drank a glass of water and headed straight to the sculpting corner where Bhumi was waiting for me. The curtains had been closed and it was a little dark. However, she had positioned enough working lights in the form of adjustable bulb lamps. I could also see that she had made special arrangements for me. She had installed a small TV on a table along the opposite wall to keep me occupied as I sat still. She had placed a food tray with snacks and fruit juices in another corner.

'So? Shall we begin?' Bhumi asked softly.

I nodded in response.

'The shirt and vest need to be taken off, please,' she said smiling, and added, 'Today, it will take slightly longer than the last time. I hope you're prepared?'

I smiled back at her. The palettes and scrapers, spatulas, cutters, knives, loose wires, wire gauze, scalpels, broom brushes and a variety of sandpapers had been laid out neatly near the wheel stand on the central workstation. Bhumi also wore a set of magnifying glasses.

'So, this is how it all begins,' she said unveiling a raw structure of a human half-figure in oil-based clay set over a wheel stand. It was an outline of a face, neck and torso. The limbs had been left out quite artistically.

'I made it with the help of measurements taken last time. It has a thick aluminium wire frame inside it, stuffed with crumpled paper and aluminium foil, secured tightly with packaging tape. This is the skeletal support on which clay has been spread. It doesn't look anything like you, right?' she said.

The body dimensions of the clay replica were almost the same as mine, albeit without the details. It was a liberating feeling to see a piece of art, completely dedicated to me. I felt as if Bhumi was creating a new Shekhar with each stroke of her hand!

I wasn't required to sit as still as a painting model but nevertheless, she did not allow me out of her sight. Bhumi looked carefully and felt my head, face, neck, chest and shoulder blades every now and then, at times using different sizes of callipers. I sat facing her, beside the sculpting wheel, on the workstation. I could see her fingers and hands dance delicately all over the clay, in soft strokes. She carefully transferred each crevice and the position of details of my face and torso on to the clay structure. She spread little heaps of clay here and there, around the eyebrows, nose, lips, ears, cheekbones, collar bones and more. With spatulas and scrapers, she flattened the structures just as she dug scalpels, knives, cutters, wire-end stems into the clay to carve out the details. She also kept playing with the lights and shadows, first over my face and then over the clay model. I was in complete submission to her as she kept adjusting my seating angle in close coordination with the positioning of the clay model.

She looked divine! For the first time, I noticed her powerful and deep eyes. Indeed, I had missed seeing her the week before. My gaze hovered all over her body. She wasn't the regular voluptuous woman my manly instincts had fancied till then. And yet, the desire I felt for her was intense, something I had never felt before.

She had tied up her curly hair tightly with a scarf. Her facial features were exceptionally sharp on her oval face. Her dusky skin was bright and glowing. I felt tempted to straighten out the frown between her eyebrows and plant a loving kiss there. Her chest rose and fell softly with her slow and steady breathing. She was dressed in a simple half-sleeved off-white top and long gypsy-blue skirt. Her cleavage was clearly visible, whenever she bent down. I caught myself trying to imagine her bare bosom, in all its softness. Her slender waist was further accentuated by the apron belt that was tied tightly around it.

Every now and then, she would shake me out of my trance-like state with her abrupt hand movements over my torso. Although her cold hands were smeared in clay, rubbing alcohol and mineral oil, my skin longed for more of her touch.

And then, I suddenly realized that it was evening already. Hours had passed like minutes.

Very broadly, the clay replica had begun to resemble my body structure. I could see my hairline, my forehead, my nose, lips, cheeks, neck, shoulder, my chest and my back reflected in the raw structure.

After a while, Bhumi sighed deeply and said, 'Phew! This is all I can do in one day!'

I adjusted my body and replied, 'Well done! Is this it?'

'Oh, no, no, no! This is the primary model. There are several layers of detailing still left. This is just the first one. We still have to work on the next level of details.'

Then she paused before speaking again, 'Listen, I have a

favour to ask. Would it be possible for you to come here every afternoon? For the next three or four days, please? Oh, please?'

'I see,' I replied, deep in thought.

'The clay model is at a very crucial stage and it would be difficult for me to work on it if there are too many gaps.'

At once, I agreed to her sincere request. For the next few afternoons, I began to sneak into her suite, largely unnoticed.

That afternoon is still vivid in my mind. The clay replica had almost been completed. The sculpture seemed to be her best work among the ones displayed in the room. The intricate details of my body seemed to have been carved from her sweat and blood as she brushed and polished the sculpture with baby oil and chamois leather. I had never seen my reflection like this, so masculine and so strong—almost like a Roman God.

It seemed like an ode from Bhumi to me. I felt worshipped. In the process of making my clay look-alike, she had transformed me from within. She had touched me somewhere deep inside and the feeling was there to stay forever. I had begun to appreciate the subtle aspects of art and creativity. I felt proud of my existence and my achievements, however small. I felt grateful for my experiences, both happy and painful, for each had a role to play in shaping me. I realized that I had been lucky to not only survive but to have been able to make it on my own, for there were many others who were still waiting to find their way.

Bhumi was adding final strokes to my clay torso, especially around the dagger stab scar that she had made to resemble the one on the right side of my chest, under the collar bone. She was using an alcohol torch to soften the clay and rework some portions of it.

'Is today the final sitting?' I asked, fearing it would be my last meeting with Bhumi in Suite 1020.

'I hope so! You have been so tolerant with me, Shekhar. I don't have enough words to thank you,' Bhumi replied. Then, she added softly, 'Making sculptures is my life. And I can't thank you enough for being a part of it. Did you enjoy this journey as much as I did?' she looked lovingly at me, or so I thought.

'More so than you,' I gave her an honest reply.

We had tea and cookies together before I got up to leave.

'Thank you for the wonderful sculpture! I shall come here tomorrow to take a final look at it,' I announced before closing the door as I left.

Upon reaching my little shanty that I called home back then, I packed a small gift for her. It was my late mother's Kashmiri pashmina shawl. Sleep deserted me that night and I lay awake planning for the next day. It was meant to be our last private meeting. But why was I sad? Perhaps I had gotten used to seeing her every day. Should I tell her about my deep longing for her company? What will she think of me? I was merely her artistic inspiration—a male muse. What if the muse had begun to love his artist? Could a muse ever demand a slice of affection from the life of the artist? Amid all the questions and counter-questions, I searched for answers without success. Finally, I fell asleep.

The next morning, I reached the hotel for work as usual. I had given breakfast a miss since I wasn't feeling hungry. I, along with my colleagues, noticed that I had replaced my gregarious charm with a quieter self.

And then, as I walked towards the lounge bar, something totally unexpected happened...

◆

'Hi, Gauri! You haven't gone home yet?' One of my office

colleagues called out from a distance. He was getting into his car when he spotted Shekhar and me, sitting together on the wooden bench in the parking lot.

'No. But I am just about to leave,' I answered.

'Need a ride somewhere?'

'Thanks, but I don't need it.'

I waved at my colleague as he drove out of the parking lot. I was annoyed with the sudden intrusion. But Shekhar seemed unperturbed. He sat on the bench, still staring at the ground.

'I am sorry, Shekhar. He is a little nosy, you know!'

I tried to nudge him to resume his story, 'So, what did you see in the hotel that morning, Shekhar?'

Shekhar leaned back on the bench and continued narrating his account, this time in a low and painful voice.

'All of Bhumi's clay sculptures were lying half packed at the lobby corridor landing. Huge sealed boxes labelled 'Mr/Mrs Trigunesh Kumar' had been piled carefully in one corner. A middle-aged gentleman, perhaps one of Mr Trigunesh Kumar's trusted personal assistants, was supervising all the packing and transportation of items that came out of Suite 1020.'

'So, Bhumi was checking out of the hotel?' I asked in dismay.

Shekhar replied, 'Bhumi had already left the hotel the night before. I was told that her father-in-law had died and she had to rush back to attend his funeral with her husband. They were scheduled to stay back in their hometown to sort out a few business matters and legal formalities. Shoolin Industries was a huge business house and Trigunesh Kumar's father had left behind a mammoth legacy to manage.'

'Bhumi must have returned after sometime?' I asked.

'No. Bhumi never came back to the hotel. From what I heard, Shoolin Industries got divided among many claimant relatives of the Kumar clan. It became difficult for Mr Trigunesh Kumar to retain the same glory. Not that the Kumars went bankrupt, but clearly, the business had stagnated, with their social status standing precariously over past accolades.'

'And what about Bhumi? Didn't you try to get in touch with her?'

'Yes. I accessed the hotel records and tried calling her on the phone number mentioned in it. I also sent her a carefully written letter. In those days, cell phones and internet were unheard of. I wasn't sure where she had gone since their ancestral property had also been sold off. After many years of search, I finally gave up and accepted the turn of events as another cruel blow to my fate.'

After a long pause, Shekhar resumed, 'For years, I remained confused and disillusioned with her sudden disappearance. At times, I wondered if she ever felt anything special for me or was I just a muse? Or was she incapable of loving anybody for that matter? She had left me so suddenly that her memories continue to haunt me, till date. As she left me, so did my worldly aspirations. The desire for better money, career and fame, all vanished. I simply wished to continue my work at the lounge bar for the rest of my life as I was waiting for Bhumi's unexpected entry one more time! It never happened. Slowly, I have reconciled with my situation, but it seems destiny has something else in store for me, yet again.'

All of a sudden, Shekhar burst into tears. His shaky hands were pressed against his face. I hugged him loosely and placed my chin over his head. Despite my asking him repeatedly, he was unable to answer further. Never had I expected to see him weep like a child, so inconsolably.

After a few minutes, he pulled himself back from me gently and stretched his white t-shirt hard to reveal a scar below his right collar bone. I realized that it must be the same dagger stab scar that he had described earlier.

The scar was slightly elongated and ran downwards. The light coloured skin over it was tight and shiny in appearance. A thin dark border surrounded the scar.

Abruptly, Shekhar got up and began to walk towards the taxi stand. Refusing any further assistance from me, he said, 'Sorry to leave in such haste, Gauri. But I am not driving myself today; I am taking home a taxi.'

'Please take care of yourself, Shekhar. But at least tell me what happened today?' I asked in a concerned voice.

He looked at me with tearful eyes and said, 'Visit the clay sculpture exhibition at the ballroom tomorrow. You shall ask no more!'

Shekhar's parting words kept ringing in my ears. I couldn't have waited till the next day. That very evening, dressed in my casual clothes, I began walking towards the hotel from the guest entrance side. With quick steps, I reached the ballroom in no time at all.

The banquet board displayed outside the ballroom mentioned:

Art Exhibition & Auction

Clay Sculptures by Late Mrs Bhumija Kumar

|| All proceeds towards 'Northern Roots Foundation' ||

(Organized by Shri Trigunesh Kumar
in loving memory of his wife)

So the artist was gone? Without as much as a fond adieu to her muse?

I entered the crowded ballroom and began to walk amid

the clay sculptures on display. The pieces were in varying shades of the same earthen colour. This time, I seemed to appreciate the art more intimately. And then, I noticed the scar, the same scar I had seen just moments before.

Shekhar!

Each sculpted piece bore the same dagger wound that Shekhar had revealed on his chest, just a while back. Be it in grief or joy, anger or cheer, intrigue or boredom, fear or courage, love or hate, the figures in clay had been set in Shekhar's timeless image of his youth. But one had to be mindful about it and look beyond the monotones of the same earthen colour. It was as easy to miss finding Shekhar in the myriad of sculptures as it was to notice him.

What brilliant artistry!

Just then, everyone seemed to move towards the auction corner to occupy the seats arranged neatly in rows. I joined them and sat on one of the chairs in the last row.

An aging gentleman stood up from among the audience, walked up to the auction platform to announce the bids open. He introduced himself as Mr Trigunesh Kumar. He also read a small speech from a piece of paper stored carefully in his hands.

'To all the gracious ladies and gentlemen sitting here for the auction, please accept my heartfelt gratitude. I stand here today, not just as Trigunesh Kumar, but also as the widowed husband of an immensely talented woman, Bhumija.

It was Bhumija's final wish to have all her work auctioned in support of 'Northern Roots Foundation', a social organization that she founded with me two years back to sustain the displaced youth of Kashmir. The foundation works towards rehabilitating young boys and girls by offering them free counselling and healthcare options, training and job placements. It also guarantees soft loans in partnership with rural banks to budding entrepreneurs.

My late wife shared a special bond with this hotel. And it was here that she desired that the auction take place. She often said this place had truly blessed her with a lifetime of art. I distinctly remember the mature transition her sculptures had made during our stay here. Lifeless human figures in clay suddenly turned alive. The clay faces gave out real tears and smiles, just as each muscle on the torso throbbed with energy.

One question, however, always intrigued the ardent admirers of Bhumija's art—what do the scars on the clay figures mean? Well, I regret to inform you that it shall always remain a mystery, even to me. But having shared a large part of my life in her company, let me try making a few honest guesses. Perhaps her fascination with human scars signifies her own wounds that she faced in this lifetime. An orphaned childhood, a forever busy husband, a barren womb, relapsing episodes of blood cancer... As I said before, I can only guess.

As I mourn her death, I also heave a sigh of relief. Bhumija no longer suffers from her mental and physical pains. She is at peace with herself and the world at large. Her legacy lives on through her art and philanthropy.

In loving memory of my wife, I hereby announce the auction open.'

As the hall began buzzing with auction clamour, I sat there quietly, guarding the answer to the big question, 'What do the scars on the clay figures mean?'

Was I the only one who knew the answer?

THE CARNAL GETAWAY

Hotels provide a great escape in which one can live out one's unfulfilled desires that include sexual fantasies as well.

I have come across many guests seeking the private comfort of hotel rooms: young executives snatching an intimate night to celebrate their new-found romance and indulge in unguarded sexuality; middle-aged managers and business owners hiring 'economy class' hookers to liberate their tired bodies from the ordinariness of work and married life; aging corporate heads and business tycoons flaunting 'business class' foreign escorts by their side to make the most of their diminishing worth and lives.

Some customers also executed well-laid out plans. Philandering wives and husbands booked interconnected rooms or at least rooms on the same floor, days in advance, to keep their extramarital romance alive. These tête-à-têtes offered convenient commitment-free liaisons along with the forbidden and, therefore, seductive taste of sex outside marriage.

A few individuals, mostly men, looked forward to release some part of sexual tension built over many episodes of watching pornographic material. Others fulfilled their sadistic and masochistic fantasies.

An elderly housekeeping staff member once removed from a room a variety of bondage items—handcuffs, thumb cuffs, rope, blindfold, leg spreader iron bar, chain, flog belt and a slave collar among other stuff. The guest had also abandoned role-play dresses—a nurse outfit and a doctor's suit. He even left behind photographs and a video recording of the racy act played out in the hotel room. It seemed as if he wished to educate the wise but blissfully ignorant room attendant about kinkiness.

As a matter of hotel policy, the finder was allowed to keep the unclaimed items after a certain period of time. In this case, the old room attendant stared at the 'prized' possessions.

Giggling co-workers began teasing him, 'Grandpa, go and have some fun with Grandma tonight!'

The senior room attendant gave them a disinterested look and replied, 'Where can I find the nearest scrap dealer? I might be able to strike a good deal for all these chains and bars.'

'But grandpa, what about the "fun" part?' Someone from the crowd prodded him again.

'Son, my wife of thirty years will not take these belts and chains lightly. I'm afraid she might turn into a true tyrant, finally. Her verbal thrashings are enough! And why should I create havoc in my one-room apartment that also shelters my sons and grandchildren?'

Everyone in the department went hysterical with laughter. Anyway, it was easy for him to pass the items through the staff security gate without being poked at as none of the guards were able to guess the *kinky* value of those scary shackles and bars.

And then, a few 'Do-It-Yourself' granddads also came visiting the hotel.

They were the quintessential aged politicians. These patriarchs would often drag their useless bodies to seek 'pubic' pleasures away from the 'public' political god-man image they had created for themselves.

Durjan Thakur, also called bhaiyya ji by his political sycophants, fit into this category seamlessly. Being the chief minister of one of the Indian states, he often visited the national capital to report important matters to the Centre. He would blend his morning-work with afternoon-pleasure before heading back home in the evening.

His short-stay room was anonymously booked as 'wash-and-change' following the orders given by the top bosses of the hotel. The junior staff always wondered, what had to be 'washed' and what had to be 'changed'?

In his personal life, bhaiyya ji had fathered three sons who went on to hold important posts in the state administration during his tenure. Reportedly, the erotic stories from his colourful past proved beyond doubt that he had enjoyed his youth to the fullest. But, now, at seventy-eight, he couldn't exert himself on the bed anymore. And yet, the hotel staff spoke about his fetish for teenage girls.

He earned a special badge among the staff—'The 'Do-It-Yourself' Granddad.

If the grapevine was to be believed, he loved to watch young girls take matters into their own hands, quite literally. He loved to watch them pleasuring themselves amid riveting moans and groans. Of course, this was only after he had nursed them long enough.

One of the outspoken 'wash-and-change' lasses had once remarked on her way out, 'Granddad could not quit his wheelchair! What bhaiyya ji actually needs is a high horsepower vacuum cleaner pipe. It might help him put some life into his old and shrivelled beam. And thanks to all the screaming, my voice-box is broken and my bottom resembles an excited female baboon's!'

It became quite a joke among female staff members who secretly giggled every time Durjan Thakur checked into the hotel.

But it wasn't always about fun and amusement. Once, I witnessed a nasty incident involving a middle-aged Arab sheikh who used to visit India to take care of his employer's shipping business. He had two wives who occasionally accompanied him during his work trips. This grave episode had threatened the reputation of the hotel and subsequent business. The discussions in the cafeteria and changing room lasted for days before the entire hotel could begin to make sense of what really happened on that occasion.

It was horrific to note the extent of brutality in human desires, when left unchecked, and the damage it could cause to its victims. What happens when one is afflicted with perverted pleasure-seeking traits that assume obsessive proportions?

Suite 1605 Sheikh Salem Ali Al Wehaibi (And Wives)

Getting drenched in the monsoon rains, lakes and houseboats, cool hill stations, luxurious train journeys, ayurveda, young masseuses at the spas, open and relaxed public spaces, ban-free alcohol, women minus the niqab, business expansion, etc. There was no dearth of excuses for the rain-starved and morally over-policed Arab natives to get away from their homeland and visit India. Overindulgence, that was despised and forbidden at home, was easy to pursue here.

The Arab visitors belonged to different countries—Qatar, Oman, Saudi Arabia, Turkey, Bahrain and Kuwait. But the majority were from the United Arab Emirates.

Arab guests are always a hotel profit-maker's delight! I could never spot a single Arab traveller with inhibited spending habits. The junior service staff often spoke of their great generosity in leaving behind large amounts of cash as tip money. They stayed longer compared to tourists from other countries. They also preferred luxury and extravagance. Be it the lavish spa treatments, exotic food festivals, and even the over-priced merchandise display at the five-star hotel shopping arcade, Arab men and women would always be there to savour it all!

One such Arab guest was Sheikh Salem Ali Al Wehaibi. The owner of a large shipping company, he began visiting India to expand their network of ports and set up new offices. He was often, but not always, accompanied by his harem consisting of two wives or at least, the second one. She was younger and he seemed to fancy her more than the older one.

The family was mostly reticent. None of the regular greetings, pleasantries or verbal expressions was used by them. Not a word was spoken to the hotel staff unless something was needed. Their facial expressions were deadpan, though they used a lot of hand gestures.

Only the Sheikh spoke on behalf of his family. He uttered short phrases in a loud voice, like, 'Come here!', 'Clean room!', 'Give Soap!', 'Extra Towel!', 'Why no shampoo in bathroom yesterday?'

All male staff members were strictly prohibited from entering the suite, especially if the wives were around. They had also been instructed never to stare at or make eye contact with the two women on the rare occasions when they stepped out of their hotel suite, always escorted by the Sheikh himself.

Other instructions included placing a copy of the Holy Quran and three prayer rugs in the bedroom. Extra coat hangers were to be stacked in the wardrobes. The executive chef had to personally guarantee that only *halal* meat was being used to cook their meals served in the suite. Sometimes, the kitchen chief would be ordered to accompany the steward carrying the food tray into the room and taste the dishes before serving it to the guests.

The Sheikh was around fifty years old. He always wore the *thobe* and *keffiyeh*. Though, once, I had spotted him wearing a pair of jeans and a t-shirt while going out for sightseeing along with his family. But that was just on one occasion.

He was tall and had a large body with a distinctly heavy neck and shoulders. He struggled to walk in the long white tunic, owing to his bulky thighs and large feet. His big arms swayed to the extent of covering the entire breadth of the corridor as he emerged from the suite, occasionally adjusting his head scarf. It was easy to hear him reach the elevators and exit the floor, even from a distance. His breathing was loud with intermittent coughing as he cleared his throat a bit too often.

Speaking aloud in a hoarse voice, he would often summon the housekeeping staff at the suite's entrance. The Sheikh would then unleash his infamous temper on the room attendants for reasons big and small, such as, closing the curtains in the sea-facing room, for folding clothes and putting them away at a different place, and even for arranging another colour of roses in the room. The food and drinks service staff faced his unprovoked wrath even for the slightest variation in the time at which he had asked them to bring the food order or clear trays.

And then, he would feel threatened if the staff didn't maintain active eye contact while listening to his chiding.

'Look at me while I talk! Okay?' used to be his pet sentence to correct them.

But it was difficult for the female staff to handle his stares, leave alone maintain a steady eye contact with the Sheikh. They would always ask for a male staff member to enter the room with them while cleaning, especially if the guest was staying by himself. Reportedly, the Sheikh made deliberate groping attempts and would sometimes brush his body against theirs when they serviced the suite. Be it the narrow bathroom door exits, the small studio kitchen or the cramped bedside area near the window, the guest just happened to follow them everywhere. One of the lady room attendants also disclosed her shock over bumping into him once. The accident happened as she was vacuuming the carpet, when he appeared right behind her, dangerously close. The lady staff would also be scared to kneel down and mop the floor or bend down to make his bed, lest he caught them unawares.

There was another secret aspect of the Sheikh that fanned the curiosity of the staff. It was his fetish for sex workers of different nationalities. He could not hide his obsession from the sharp observant eyes of the hotel concierge and security staff. They also got him billed for double room occupancy on 'those' nights.

News would spread like wildfire. The staff waited to hear from the grapevine. What had the Sheikh chosen last evening? Was she Russian, Chinese, European, African or just local Indian?

The concierge desk person used to provide the inquisitive hotel crowd with complete details and the security staff loved to endorse it! How did the hooker arrive at the hotel lobby? Did she have a passport? What was she wearing? How did she look? How old was she? How long did she stay? Was she fine at the time of leaving? Did she appear ravaged?

Security guards posted at the hotel lobby were known to bully these prostitutes and their handlers. In fact, one of them had been thrown out of his job since he took regular bribes from the prostitutes, in exchange for allowing their 'little business' inside the hotel premises. But before he left, he let out some juicy details about the Sheikh. This was based on his interactions with the sex workers waiting to be picked up by their handlers at the hotel porch.

Allegedly, the Sheikh wasn't an easy customer. The young girls had to deal with a sex maniac who often forced them to comply with his unnatural demands.

But he would sober down during the visits with his spouses. The wives, however, did not bear any similarity with him. Or even with each other. Both the ladies wore *abaya*, the traditional black covering robe, with their faces wrapped inside a niqab at all times. However, the younger wife, Nouf, dressed more liberally underneath her black robes. She wore smart tops coupled with knee-length skirts or capri pants and jeans, whereas the elder wife confined herself to wearing kaftans and long maxis or loosely stitched trousers coupled with full-sleeved shirts, at the most. Unlike Nouf, she wore black gloves and socks below the *abaya* to conceal her hands and feet from being seen by strangers during outings.

While the elder wife stayed quiet and withdrawn, Nouf liked talking to the lady staff members of the hotel. She was better educated and had practised dentistry for a while before getting married to the Sheikh. Almost half her husband's age, she had a pretty face and a slender body.

I still have vivid memories about one of my intimate conversations with Nouf. It was late afternoon. I had a relatively light working day with most of my follow-ups being completed. While strolling through the guest corridor, I found the suite door left open. The Sheikh was mostly out for work at that time of the day. Out of concern and curiosity, I knocked at the door softly and called out 'Housekeeping'. There was no response despite both the wives being present inside the suite.

I shut the door from outside and was just about to leave when the room opened. It was Nouf.

'Yes?' she enquired, all wrapped up inside a cloak made of some thick material.

'Good afternoon, ma'am! I found the room door open. Hope you are comfortable in the room?' I quickly clarified.

'Oh! I had probably not closed it well enough after the cleaning lady left,' she responded in perfect English, speaking with a clear accent, much to my astonishment. It was a welcome change after having to put up with the Sheikh's rude speech and ugly mannerisms on earlier occasions.

'That's all right, ma'am. Is there anything else we could do to make your stay more pleasant?' I offered.

'Nothing! It's quite comfortable here.'

I smiled politely and took her leave.

'Why don't you come inside? Let's talk,' Nouf tried calling me back.

I quickly turned around and grabbed the offer. One of the aspects I loved about my work was the human interaction. It was good to meet people from a wide variety of backgrounds, tastes and nationalities.

Saudi Arabia had fascinated me deeply since childhood. I found the Arabian stories delightful and the dresses depicted in the story books always caught my attention—'Aladdin's Magic Lamp', 'Ali Baba and the Forty Thieves', 'Sinbad the Sailor' and of course, 'One Thousand and One Nights'. However, I knew very little about their culture and women. And whatever I knew was based solely on storybooks, newspapers, magazines and gossip among the hotel staff.

That afternoon offered me a wonderful opportunity to interact with this beautiful young Arab lady belonging to the oppressed gender, as projected in stories and reported by media. I could not have let it pass in a million years.

I entered the suite and both of us walked towards the

sitting room that overlooked the vast blue sea. Nouf pointed towards the couch gesturing me to sit down. I hesitated a bit as a mark of respect to the in-house guest.

'Sit down! I insist,' she ordered.

There was a distinct sweet and woody fragrance in the room, part sandalwood and part amber. Nouf sensed my eagerness to know its source.

'It's *bakhoor*. Small scented bricks made of *Oud* wooden chips. It also has some natural oils and other stuff. They are burnt like incense sticks, but in a small lamp.' She pointed at a small brass burner giving out a light smoke at one corner of the sitting room.

'It looks like Aladdin's magic lamp!' I remarked, much to the amusement of the young lady.

'If you say so,' she laughed.

Staring out of the large windows, she commented, 'The sea looks delightful when it's raining. I love to see so much water.'

I politely agreed with her observation without revealing the chaos that resulted from such incessant rains, especially in crowded urban cities of India. After all, why would she want to know of choked drains, flooded basements, stolen umbrellas and delayed local trains?

The elder wife peeped into the sitting room and found us talking to each other. Before I could acknowledge her presence by standing up, she had disappeared back into her bedroom.

After a bit of closely guarded conversation, I relaxed and discussed almost everything. What began as a normal conversation about the hotel, sightseeing, food and culture in India had strayed into intense and intimate areas of discussion in less than an hour's time.

Nouf and I spoke as if there was no end to our thoughts. We discussed about education and career options for girls in the two countries, getting married and having children, the status of women and, of course, the acceptance of plural marriage or polygamy in the largely Islamic Middle East. I felt as if we had known each other long before we even met.

'Would you like to have some *bakhoor* smoke?' Nouf interrupted the conversation.

I wondered how can one 'have' smoke. Just then, she refilled the lamp with some more of the little *Oud* bricks.

'Now, watch this!' She loosened her waist belt and stepped over the burning lamp. The heat and smoke was hidden underneath her heavy cloak. She closed her eyes and took deep breaths while pulling at the drape from various places for the smoke to enter. After a few minutes, she parted her legs while standing over the burning lamp and lifted the cloak a wee bit.

This time she looked at me and smiled.

'My husband loves the smell of *Oud* all over me, especially inside me, you know, down here. You must try it once!' She said pointing at her groin.

I noticed her more closely this time and felt that she wasn't wearing a single piece of cloth below the heavy drape while 'having' the smoke. Perhaps it was a daily ritual for her to enhance her bodily looks and feel. Nouf boasted of a truly well-kept body. Her thick long black hair shimmered in the soft light pouring in from the windows. Her almond-shaped large brown eyes held the most expressive gaze. The soft and supple fair-toned skin on her face and limbs bore an even appearance. She did not show any signs of ageing in all the thirty years of her existence.

After a long spell of deep inhaling, she finally stepped away from the lamp. She returned to the sofa and sat nearer to me this time. There was a certain pink glow on her face.

'*Oud* fragrance lasts on the body for hours.'

'I have never met a more beautiful lady beside you, ma'am. I am sure your husband loves you dearly,' I remarked.

To my surprise, Nouf became very silent. The statement seemed to have made a profound effect on her.

'Well, as long as it lasts! But thank you for your kind comment.'

After a short spell of silence, she resumed, 'This is his second marriage. What about you? Are you married?'

'Yes ma'am. I got married just last year.'

'Is this your husband's first marriage?' she asked in a casual tone.

'Most definitely. We have known each other since our college days,' I may have felt a little offended at her question.

Nouf asked, 'Men don't marry more than once in India?'

'No ma'am. It's not common in the larger Indian society.'

'Hmm… But, then, how do Indian men handle their sexual desires for other women?'

'I am not sure about it, ma'am,' I tried to maintain a respectful distance.

After all, she was an esteemed guest staying at the hotel. I restrained myself from criticizing the overemphasized polygamous needs of men, lest it hurt her pride in belonging to a society that felt otherwise.

But Nouf was comfortable in exchanging notes on this intimate subject. 'Whoever said that Arab women are restrained?' I thought.

'You know, nature has given men stronger urges than us,' she said, matter-of-factly.

'But doesn't it bother you?' The words came tumbling out of my mouth, 'Ma'am,' I added carefully.

'Who am I to question the Holy Quran? The Prophet says

that a man is permitted to marry up to four times. But with the condition that he treats all his four wives equally. So I don't find anything wrong in it.'

'Aren't the wives jealous of each other?'

'Yes. But it lasts only for a few insecure moments.'

Nouf adjusted her seat, sat upright and rested her back further on the sofa. Then she continued, 'Saudi men travel, study and work abroad and it's not uncommon for them to marry outside their homeland. Now, what happens to us women who aren't allowed to travel and study like our male counterparts? In my case, I faced an acute shortage of grooms. I stayed unmarried despite nearing thirty which is a difficult situation to face for a woman in the Arab society. I yearned for marriage and to start a family of my own. Left with no option, I accepted to be a second wife rather than staying a spinster for the rest of my life.'

Although Nouf wished to speak some more, there was silence in the room. After a few minutes had passed, I prodded, 'You are an excellent communicator, ma'am. You speak so well. Why don't you start writing?'

However, she had something else racing through her mind.

Still in deep thought, Nouf asked, 'But you haven't answered my first question. How does an Indian man handle his desire for other women? Especially if he has unfulfilled desires from his wife?'

'He would go to prostitutes, I guess,' I answered.

'Ah! There you see. At least, you accept that men cannot remain stranded alone with their unmet needs?'

'Right, ma'am,' I agreed politely and, then added, 'But sex trade is still a menace here.'

'My Sheikh also calls for sex workers! That's once in a while, when he is travelling for work.'

I was shocked to discover that the Sheikh's wife knew all about his sexual escapades. And the directness with which Nouf put it was too hard-hitting.

She continued, 'What's wrong about it? Men are our providers. Some travel more than others for work. It's difficult for them to stay away from their wives and family. Then, should he marry again at his frequent place of work? Now think about this as well. A man has certain wild fantasies and desires but he respects and fears his wife and cannot make her a part of them. That is when a prostitute comes into the picture. Her services help men tide over lonely times and live their wildest dreams to the fullest. I am okay with him hiring a few prostitutes because these women have no claim over his love and attention. They just please him in exchange of a few cash notes, right? A wife, on the other hand, would be a different ball game altogether. My Sheikh is allowed two more wives. In my heart, I know that one day, I would have to share some of my Sheikh's love, attention and time with someone else who might be younger than me, just the way I took it away from his first wife and it is this thought that I have difficulty coming to terms with. I heaved a sigh of relief since Nouf had owned up to feeling jealous should there be more wives. So much for her patronising the social benefits of polygamy, I thought to myself.

A little over two hours had passed since we began our engrossing chat. I smiled and looked at my watch so she could guess my obligation to leave.

'It is so good talking to you. But do you have to go now?' she asked.

'Yes ma'am. I wish we could have talked some more, but I must report back to work. Again, I'm in awe of your candid style of speaking. You can also author a book on Arab women using your own experiences. I'm sure readers like me from other parts of the world would lap it up.'

Nouf got excited, 'Oh! You really think so? Thank you!' she exclaimed as we got up from our seats.

'I am checking out tomorrow. But let's see if I can finish writing one story before my visit next month.'

The goodbyes were done. She walked me till the door and gave me a tight hug before I left the suite.

A knowing smile persisted for a while on my face as I disappeared into the back area of the hotel. I felt deeply enriched from my thorough interaction with a person belonging to an entirely different culture.

It was time well spent, or so I thought.

♦

(A Month Later)

'What happened to you?'

I had to repeat my question many times before she could reply, choking back her tears.

'Can you call a doctor?' she said in a muffled voice.

She had wrapped a double bed cover from one of the hotel rooms tightly around her. Her back against the staircase railing, she appeared too weak to keep her head upright. With eyes half-shut, she spoke in between sobs.

I picked up my walkie-talkie and asked for Dr Nigam to be sent urgently. The telephone operator handled the task on high priority.

Meanwhile, I sent out another request, trying hard to make it sound like just another routine message.

'Security? This is Gauri from housekeeping. Please come over to the sixteenth floor staff staircase, over.'

I did not divulge any other details lest the entire night-shift staff come rushing to the spot. It wasn't a good idea to disturb the regular working of the hotel at 2 a.m. after all!

'This is Security-In-Charge Rajesh Singh. I am on my way, over.'

'See you Rajesh, over and out.'

I also briefed the duty manager, Dheeraj Rathore, who was waiting in the hotel lobby. It was essential to follow the protocol and inform any unusual event to the highest decision-making authority during night shifts.

I walked back towards the girl.

Her looks were unconventional—she had piercings on her ears, chin and nose. Her gold-streaked hair looked dry and brittle.

'Help will arrive soon. But how did you reach here?' I repeated softly.

'I escaped from the suite,' she spoke as if in great pain.

'From Suite 1605?'

She nodded.

'You escaped from the Sheikh, you mean?' I was slightly taken aback since he was visiting with Nouf.

'Yes!' She gave a loud cry. She wept inconsolably and her howls rang through the massive building.

The staff staircase area was largely deserted during the wee hours of the morning. Thankfully, the noise and attention did not attract any onlookers.

Knowing that she had escaped from the Sheikh didn't surprise me. But all the nauseating stories about the Sheikh that I had overheard in the hotel cafeteria and changing room came rushing back to haunt me. Was this for real? For some time, I used to give the benefit of the doubt to the Sheikh, assuming that my colleagues loved to exaggerate his sexual escapades to spice up their dull working hours.

But, apparently, the concierge and the security guards weren't lying after all! My struggle to calm her continued. I crouched down next to her and placed my hand over her shoulder, but it only worsened her outburst.

'What exactly happened to you?' I asked as I was still unsure about the details.

In response, she loosened the bedcover wrapped around her body and tried to sit upright. Then, she opened the bedcover folds revealing her chest.

I gasped in fear and stumbled backwards. What I saw was more brutal than anything I had ever witnessed before. My worst nightmares were mild compared to the horrific picture that lay bare in front of me.

'SHIT! SHIT! SHIT!' I couldn't stop uttering the coarse words relentlessly. It seemed as if my mind attempted to relieve itself of the disgust through my mouth.

I noticed that parts of her bosom were missing. The nipples had been torn off from her breasts. The peaks were not bleeding but were tipped bright-red. However, the blood-stained bedcover indicated that the cuts must have bled profusely.

'He bit off my flesh. Can you believe it?' she asked incredulous, 'He bit off my flesh!' she cried out.

I had gone blank. Nervously, I sat beside her and held her hands, squeezing them tightly. I wanted to give her a hug too but I was too scared of hurting her further.

Flashes of Nouf crossed my mind. Was she there when all this happened? Was I confused? Had she even accompanied the Sheikh this time? I doubted myself as I was beyond tired as a result of continued night shifts.

I heard the fast approaching footsteps on the staircase down below. A clanking sound could also be heard as someone opened the service elevators. I carefully covered her bare chest with the bedcover again. To my relief, help had arrived from all sides. The Duty Manager arrived with the news that Dr Nigam was scheduled to reach the hotel in another fifteen minutes. Rajesh Singh rushed towards us to assess what had happened and how best the hotel security could help, if any need arose.

'Please arrange for a wheelchair, Rajesh. She must lie flat on a bed in one of the vacant rooms on this floor,' I spoke hurriedly.

'Gauri, please don't panic!' Mr Rathore gave me a rather stern look, 'We will obviously shift her into one of the hotel rooms, if needed. But, first of all, I have to understand what's happening here?'

Dheeraj Rathore was an experienced middle-aged hotel manager. He had began his career as a humble hotel cashier in the same hotel, almost seventeen years back. His hard-work, networking skills and fierce loyalty to the hotel brand had helped him overcome several barriers. He had reached a senior position when his co-workers from his hotel-joining days were, at the most, still senior cashiers or bell desk supervisors. On the contrary, I was just a fresh management graduate. It was perfectly justified for him to ask questions before the next course of action could be decided.

Mr Rathore and Rajesh listened to me carefully as I described the circumstances under which I found the injured girl. I also shared with them the allegations she had made against the Sheikh. My voice trembled to describe her terrible wounds and the pain that she was in.

I spewed with hate and anger.

'The Sheikh must be severely punished under the law for what he did to this girl. If you listen to the informal discussions among our staff, you would realize that his cruel perversions have hurt many other sex workers in the past. But this time he has gone too far—'

'Gauri!' Mr Rathore stopped me abruptly, 'We shall talk about this later. Don't jump to conclusions! We will do whatever is right. First, this girl needs medical attention. Dr Nigam will be here to take care of that. But let's not forget that above everything else lies the fragile reputation of the hotel.'

Then he turned towards Rajesh, 'Stay here till further instructions. And Gauri, you must continue with your shift as you are the only female manager available at this hour. Call for a wheelchair on standby. Let the girl be shifted in the presence of Dr Nigam.'

Just before leaving the spot, he looked at us firmly in the eye and ordered, 'Send someone to Suite 1605 to remove her belongings—clothes, purse, any other stuff. I am going to make a call to the guest and meet him. You can keep me posted about her condition through the reception.'

He disappeared into the sixteenth floor guest corridor.

By then, almost an hour had passed.

The girl was lying quietly with a white towel over her waist. Perhaps the heavy concoction of painkillers and other medicines had worked. Or maybe it was the comforting presence of Dr Nigam. He had assured her that her wounds would heal properly and the scars could be hidden with reconstructive surgery, which was expensive but effective.

'Do you feel better now?' I asked the girl.

She merely nodded.

I was alone with her in the room now. I could see her frail body with tattoos on the sides. Some initials inked in a weird font ran from below the armpits and continued all along till the ankles on her dry and pale skin.

With her eyes closed, she spoke in whispers.

'He acted as if I was some disgusting creature, full of dirt. Like, I had arrived unsolicited. The minute I entered, he asked me to undress and clean myself. I felt so scared but I trusted my boss, who is also my ex-boyfriend. I had faith in his decision to send me here. I tried to assure myself. Maybe he is from a different country, so, it's hard to understand his mannerisms. Even though I was not completely sure, I still complied with his demands.'

'He stood at the bathroom door as I showered. He ordered me to apply soap all over. Then, as I stood there drenched and lathered, he ran his hands all over me. With cold eyes, he pushed his fingers abruptly inside me. He kept shouting, "Keep clean! Keep clean!" I had barely wrapped a towel around myself when he pulled me by my hair and took me to a scent-smoking lamp in one of the bedrooms. He asked me to stand over the burning lamp with my legs spread apart. Soon, he asked me to squat over the lamp. My legs began hurting after a few minutes and I may have fidgeted. He became upset. He squeezed my left arm hard and pulled me up sharply. I stood facing the wall, bending forward from my waist. "Bend down! Bend down!" he roared again. I watched him pick up the smoking lamp and turn towards me. My groin almost burned as he scrambled like a beast trying to insert the tip of that burning lamp inside me. I realized the danger of being alone in the company of this twisted customer. So I tried to wriggle out of his tight hold. Perhaps he sensed my intention to escape. He locked my arms, turned me over, and pushed me against the wall. I saw that savage look in his eyes before he began gnawing at my neck. Despite all my fear and pain, I stood still, not knowing what to do—should I scream out, charge at him or simply run away? How was that going to help? How could I have walked out of the room bare-bodied?

There I was, locked inside the biggest suite of the hotel with a ferocious animal. By now, he had reached for my chest. Before I could understand what was happening, he tore off my breasts with his bare teeth. One after the other! At that moment, he resembled a hungry wolf with blood smeared all over his mouth. Fearing for my life, I kicked him hard and pushed him away. I ran towards the door naked. On my way out, I pulled the bedcover along with me. Nothing that I had left in the room mattered, clothes, jewellery, purse, money, not even the torn pieces of my flesh.'

Tears trickled through her closed eyes as she went quiet again, perhaps wanting to sleep. There was a sudden knock on the door. It was Rajesh. He brought a message from Mr Rathore. I was free to resume my shift since another lady was present in the hotel. I nodded and stepped out of the room. It was only after I glanced back at the injured girl that I realized that I hadn't even asked her name.

I noticed that many people had gathered outside the room.

On one side, an intense discussion ensued between Mr Rathore and a tall robust man with tattoos all over his neck and arms. On the other side, the Sheikh kept peeping out of the slightly open door of his suite. Nouf was still missing. Two security guards were pacing up and down the guest floor corridor.

'Excuse me! I have to go inside,' a voluptuous middle-aged woman nudged me away from the door. She was dressed in a black top and jeans with a black leather coat. She had bleached hair and her face was made-up with glittery coatings of face powder and a bright red lipstick.

'But, who are you, miss?' I asked.

'I am with her,' she disappeared inside the room banging the door in my face. Her cheap perfume still lingered in the corridor. I turned to Rajesh. He nodded to confirm that she was indeed with the wounded girl asleep inside.

Mr Rathore signalled me to carry on with my other duties. His lips uttering 'Thank you!' could be read from a distance. On my way back to the housekeeping office, I spotted two policemen standing in the hotel lobby. However, I wasn't sure if they had visited the hotel on account of the Sheikh.

◆

'So! How's she doing now?' I asked Rajesh as he sat across from me at one of the staff cafeteria tables.

Rajesh gave me a blank look, took a sip from his teacup and answered vaguely, 'The tea served during night shift isn't as good as the morning one.'

I frowned, still staring at him.

'What?' he whispered, pretending to watch the wall-mounted television placed in the farthest corner of the cafeteria.

Unable to handle my gaze for too long, he answered, 'I have no idea about her.'

'What do you mean? She was still in the hotel last night.'

'Yes. But the handler along with his assistant whisked her away soon after you left.'

'Where have they taken her?'

'Why do you ask me?' Rajesh's discomfort was obvious.

'How do you expect me to know where whores live? Such girls are very well aware of the consequences before entering the trade,' he spoke with disgust.

I turned quiet.

After a while he spoke again, 'Stuff like this happens. You'll also get used to it in good time.'

'But wasn't the Sheikh arrested by the police?'

'He and his servile wife have already checked out from the hotel this evening. They must be halfway home by now.'

'Really!' I remarked loudly.

'Not without paying the fine, of course. It cost him dearly. He had to dole out huge sums of cash for the two policemen to dump his case. Next, he paid the handler to make up for the lost business and cover the medical treatment of his injured worker.'

I watched him take another sip of tea.

'It's in the best interest of all! If reported, such incidents can damage the hotel's reputation profoundly. By the way, the Sheikh has been blacklisted in our hotel. We'll not see him again.'

'No reaction from his wives, especially the young one?'

'From what I hear, the younger wife was fully aware of her husband's perversions. She was also present in the suite, all along. She never did anything about it, though. Strange, isn't it? How these women turn a blind eye to the depravations of their husbands!'

'Hmm...I know,' I murmured, without letting out even a hint of the close interaction I had had with Nouf a month back and how disturbed I had felt about her reported submissiveness.

Tea-break was over.

I couldn't stop myself from visiting Suite 1605. What was I looking for? Maybe some answers?

The sixteenth floor guest corridor was quiet and looked peaceful. All the chaos from the previous night had died down.

I rang the doorbell and softly announced "housekeeping". Was I expecting someone to open the door? Maybe, Nouf? I wished she was there to explain everything, one last time.

I opened the room with my housekeeper keys. There was

a dark lull in the room. Traces of *Oud* still haunted the place.

It was easy to figure out that the Sheikh had left in a hurry. There were two half-eaten meal plates on the food tray, the washbasin tap was slightly open, wet towels were thrown near the bathroom entrance, luggage rack was turned upside down, hangers were tossed on the bed. One piece of a forgotten pair of stilettos lay blocking the entrance to one of the bedrooms. But where was the other one?

I began walking towards the bedroom. I ignored the view from the sitting room windows. The perfect cityscape reflecting on the seawaters couldn't distract me tonight.

In the farthest corner, I found the *bakhoor*. But this time the lamp was broken. Or maybe it had been crushed mercilessly? Ashes were strewn on the floor, all around it.

And beside it lay the other stiletto, its heel broken into bits and pieces.

Yes! Nouf had replied, after all.

...WHO BECAME A 'REBEL EXECUTIVE'

Gauri, the trained manager reaches the country's capital! The timid girl has made way for a forthright woman who enjoys her independent status in one of the largest Indian metros. A woman who loves shopping, watching movies and partying with friends and is in her first throes of romance in a new marriage.

She has important duties such as handling VIP guests, night shifts, floor renovations, preparing duty rosters, collating departmental budgets, making training calendars and writing standard operating procedures.

But she no longer tries to please everyone at work. Her softer middle class approach has become more balanced. Though years of training, working on double shifts and encounters with few arrogant guests have built a sense of growing dissatisfaction within her.

She shares some more stories...

DIPLO-MAZEY!

What comes to my mind when I think of politicians and state-sponsored events? Stifling protocol? Condescending attitudes? Or the accompanying intrusive security checks?

I have had bittersweet encounters with seductively polished but cynical representatives from foreign embassies, snooty nit-picking personal assistants of politicians and bureaucrats, and a horde of mostly silent but forever agitated special security guards, such as black cat commandos, SPG teams, BSF jawaans and state police constables.

And yes, I do understand that they all were doing their own jobs, but I was also supposed to be doing mine, which frequently came into direct conflict with theirs.

One such event still stands out strongly in my mind. There was a foreign delegation staying at the hotel for three days when the prime minister from one of the neighbouring nations came to visit India. The concourse was planned in a bid to improve trade and political cooperation between both the countries. My humble little professional world of the hotel was nowhere a match to the profoundness of the situation. But my insignificant world seemed to be the first to get deeply impacted by it!

Weeks before the meeting, all the rooms on the two topmost elite guest floors were blocked off because of the impending visit. The finest and largest hotel suite was set aside for the prime minister's arrival. The reception staff was facing the wrath of regular guests as they kept refusing them entry into the best floors. Although no fresh bookings or check-ins were being accepted, the long-staying guests could not be shifted from their residences on those elite floors. We watched the general manager and departmental heads fuss over the preparations endlessly.

◆

21 February 2003 (the job begins)

I reported for work as usual at the housekeeping department. The log book had a rather copious entry made by my boss which read:

Date	Log Book Entry	Sign
21/02/03	In preparation for the foreign delegation visit from 26 to 28 Feb, all managers and supervisors are hereby requested to read the following carefully and sign: 1. No weekly offs or leaves will be given between 26/02/03 and 01/03/03. This applies to all managers, supervisors, hotel staff as well as contract staff. 2. Kindly bring and carry at all times, a proof of your identity—PAN card, driving license or passport, every day from 26 to 28 Feb. This is compulsory. 3. Please wear clean uniform and be well-groomed for the high-profile foreign delegation visit.	
(to be read out to all morning, afternoon & night shift staff)		

A neatly folded paper printout was also pinned carefully to

the log book page. I opened it and found a forwarded copy of an email exchange between the hotel sales manager and the civil administration.

—Forwarded Message—

From: Room Sales Manager [thebluecollar@best-esthotels.com]
Sent: Thursday, 20 February 2003 4:16 PM
To: 'Head–Housekeeping'; 'Head–Kitchens'; 'Head–Front Office'; 'Head–Food & Beverage Service'
Cc: General Manager [thebigboss@best-esthotels.com]
Subject: FOREIGN DELEGATION VISIT–26 to 28 February 2003

—Original Message—

From: Protocol Assistant [thewhitecollar@bureaucracy.in]
Sent: Thursday, 20 February 2003 4:10 PM
To: Room Sales Manager [thebluecollar@best-esthotels.com]
Subject: Refer to Communication No. 000013456YPPP/213/03

Etiquette Cell @ Bureaucracy
ABC Avenue, XYX Sector, State Capital-000001, India
Phone: 0888-888888,
E-mail: thewhitecollar@bureaucracy.in
Website: www.etiquettecell.in

No. SSAAS/167/2003/   Dated: 20-02-2003

From: Shri Etiquette Master,
Protocol Assistant, Etiquette Cell, India
ABC Avenue, XYX Sector, State Capital-000001, India
Phone: 0888-888888,
E-mail: thewhitecollar@bureaucracy.in,
Website: www.etiquettecell.in

To: The Room Sales Manager
Best-est Hotels
E-mail: thebluecollar@best-esthotels.com

> Dear Mr Blue Collar,
> This is to inform you that you shall be receiving all the details of members, arrival and departure details, and stay requirements for the delegation through AAHHG-courier (consignment tracking code: AAHHG1009876). The document must be reaching you by tomorrow. However, please note the dates as 26–28 February 2003. Kindly acknowledge this communication, and return two printed and signed copies of this email by fastest courier.
>
> Warm Regards,
> Etiquette Master
>
> (Shri White Collar, Indian Etiquette Services)
> Protocol Assistant
> Etiquette Cell, India

Somehow, the clutter of unnecessary words not only defied the five W's of communication that were taught during management training, but also appeared like a complete mockery of my humble internet intelligence. In a desperate attempt, I tried looking for a relevant message in the jumble of formal ramblings.

I could spot only one useful piece of information. It was the mention of the delegation dates—26–28 February 2003.

◆

25 February 2003 (the job gets done)
 'Finally, the day has ended!'
 I comforted myself as I entered the service elevators from the guest corridor on the eighth floor. The floor staff comprising of room attendants, housemen, florists, carpet cleaners, tailor, upholsterer, kenfixit (engineering and maintenance rep) and chandelier cleaners accompanied me. It was almost 9 p.m. and we were all tired from working on a double shift since

seven in the morning. I had been made incharge of the eighth floor and it was my responsibility to overlook the comfort and needs of the foreign delegates who were expected to check in the next day.

We were very pleased with ourselves and felt proud of the perfect guest floor we had managed to create. The guest corridor carpet had been shampooed and combed, the ceiling corners were stain-free and clean, the lights sparkled bright and the passage smelt divinely fresh from the carnations and rose flower arrangements that were delicately placed upon the credenza in front of the guest elevator.

The general manager and departmental heads were satisfied with the quality of rooms that had been prepared under my charge. Apart from a few minor observations, there were generous accolades meted out to me and my team. Each room had been attended to in great detail, first by the kenfixit to make sure everything worked—bulbs, electrical points, hair dryers, mini bar, smooth drawers, window panels, hot water and cold water taps, and bath tub stoppers. Subsequently, the rooms had been spring cleaned and scrubbed—the carpets, upholstery, lamp shades, lights and chandeliers, bathroom fixtures, water closet and washbasin—with care over a period of four days by an army of hotel staff. The linen and towelling used on bed and bathroom had been procured and specially prepared for these rooms. Finally, little bowl arrangements of pink Dutch roses embellished the surroundings further.

I thanked my team for their wholehearted efforts and wished them luck for the next day. I warned the night shift staff not to mess around with the guest rooms or the guest corridor on the eighth floor. After the final debriefing session, I also left for the day to catch up on some sleep at home.

♦

26 February 2003 (the job gets undone, to be redone)

I dabbed on some extra face powder to hide the dark circles around my tired eyes and applied matte maroon-coloured lipstick generously. I draped the crisp silk uniform sari with utmost care and tied my hair neatly into a bun. I pushed the pager into its cover, and fixed it onto my waist. Clutching my duty diary, I checked myself in the mirror one last time. Perfect!

It was exactly 7.30 a.m. by the wall clock which hung in the executive ladies' locker room and I was ready for the big day. The foreign delegates on my guest floor were expected to check in between 9.30 am and 10 a.m. After a quick breakfast at the staff canteen, I reached the department to make sure that the staff had reported perfectly groomed and carried their identity cards, as had already been briefed to them days in advance. Being incharge of the eighth floor, I led the floor staff as we went upstairs. We smiled at each other and focused on the day ahead like soldiers marching towards the battlefield.

The service elevators opened in front of us.

Lo and behold!

Who welcomed us but a fleet of sniffer dogs with their state police handlers?

Good lord!

The yellow Labradors growled momentarily at the sound of the opening and closing of the service elevator doors and then continued with their loud panting.

Shocked by this unexpected sight, we entered the floor pantry on the left side where cleaning trolleys, vacuum cleaners, linen and other guest supplies were stored. The pantry had been thoroughly ransacked in the name of inspection.

For a minute, I stopped to check if we were indeed on the same eighth floor which we left last night. It was a mixed feeling of anger and disbelief to think how easily someone had raided our territory without showing any respect for the effort that had gone into setting it up.

At the door leading to the guest corridor from the back area, a mysterious looking temporary walk-in security gate had been installed which beeped, involuntarily, every ten seconds.

A stern policeman manned the exit door with a handheld detector-cum-beeper. He did a body-check of everybody entering the floor which made everyone uncomfortable. However, it gave him a reason to stand there, in the thick of action, instead of being stationed in the back area, away from the limelight. It wasn't hard to figure out the boredom they must face despite being in the high-profile surroundings.

The room attendants mustered up some courage and gathered together their cleaning trolleys and towelling materials from the ravaged pantry. As usual, they lined up to enter the guest corridor to begin their day.

'Stop! Please identify yourselves!' The armed guards near the temporary security-check gate prohibited the hotel staff from entering the guest corridor. 'Please walk through the gate and get your equipments checked by the guards. Keep your identity cards ready. You will also be issued with special duty cards and your movements will be monitored. Please report to the guard sitting here whenever you leave or enter this floor. Any doubts?'

All of us nodded our heads. Senior room attendants, with clean service records of twenty-five years, appeared slightly confused with the sudden scepticism being shown towards their identity. Nevertheless, they sportingly displayed their ration cards, driving licenses, passports, etc. The walk-in security-check gate kept beeping endlessly from all the keys dangling from the bodies of the room attendants which visibly irritated the guards. Anyway, the cleaning trolleys and buckets were meticulously brushed over with metal detectors.

Finally, the housekeeping staff was allowed entry into the guest floor.

I stood there for a while. Then, I started walking along the corridor, looking inside the rooms. It was nothing short of horrifying. Each room lay mercilessly raided; a far cry from their state the previous day when they had been prepared with diligence. Every single room was open and different kinds of special duty personnel were walking in and out of the doors. A few of them were recognizable since they were in uniforms, but I could barely identify others who were mostly in safari suits which was a common attire worn by thousands of bureaucrats. It consists of a generally tan-coloured pair of trousers and matching half-sleeve shirt. A closer look at the special duty cards revealed that most of the safari suits were actually worn by the Indian staff at the foreign embassy and also the Indian ministry.

Hardly an hour was left for the foreign delegation guests to arrive. The floor staff shared their distress with me over the plundered state of the rooms. Beds had been turned upside down, heavy furniture had been displaced, flower vases had been upturned, fruits were squished, mini bar doors had been left ajar, towels had been thrown into bathtubs, shoe imprints and dog paw marks were all over the bathroom floors, and many toiletries were missing. A few patrolmen had even used the guest toilets under the veil of security room checks.

A few moments later, I spotted a distinguished middle-aged officer on duty. He was standing towards the end of the guest corridor, formally dressed in a greyish-blue suit and light green tie. Most of the duty personnel seemed to be reporting back to him on almost every matter and waiting for his nod of approval. He displayed fine mannerisms but lacked even the slightest hint of a smile on his pensive face. Wading through the chaotic crowd of special duty staff, I went up to him to express my concern over the dilapidated state of the rooms and the impending arrival of the foreign delegates. I decided that I would be direct and fearless in my communication with him. After all, neither was I reporting to him nor was he on the list of the esteemed foreign delegation.

He was wearing a badge around his neck that read 'Hiten Mediratta, Protocol Officer—On Special Duty'.

'He must be "special" for these lesser mortals who are running around haphazardly on the guest floor but not for me,' I thought, thoroughly disgusted with the security treatment meted out to the lovingly-prepared guest rooms under my supervision.

'Hi!' I said to him. 'I would like to know when these security checks are likely to get over. Actually, there is very little time left for us to redo the guest rooms. They are in pretty bad shape at the moment.'

'All in good time, my dear lady! Why are you so anxious?' Mr Mediratta replied in a rather patronizing fashion. He came closer to read my uniform name tag.

'Hmmm... Gauri, is that right? Are you in charge of this floor?' Mr Mediratta enquired.

'Yes, I am,' I replied abruptly.

'Arre madam, all the hotel staff must address him as "sir", please! He is senior to all of us here,' one of the aging special duty staff members retorted, speaking in poorly-accented English. The elderly man appeared to be one of those quintessential junior employees nearing job retirement and thus retorting to desperate subservience towards senior officers in a last ditch attempt to rise up the ranks.

I swallowed my pride, smiled and said, 'Oh, I see. Good that you corrected me. Yes, "sir!" I am the floor incharge.'

'Good! Actually, I was looking for you since there's a small task I need you to do. While the rooms are getting tidied up, could you replace the welcome kits that my staff had placed earlier with fresh folders?' said Mr Mediratta. He turned to the same sycophantic staff member who had corrected me earlier, 'Gupta ji, can you get me two samples of each of the welcome kit sets?'

'Ji Sir, in a minute!' Gupta ji raced away to get the samples. One could see the sad state of his worn out grey safari suit hanging over his weak frame.

Meanwhile, I reasserted the importance of having the guest floor vacated by the special duty staff from the ministry as well as the foreign embassies. 'Sir, forty-five minutes are not enough for turning around twenty rooms. If you don't hand over the floor right away, I am afraid the high-profile delegates might have to wait in the lobby while the rooms are being cleaned,' I said, almost threatening Mr Mediratta.

'Oh! Then, let me speak with the people concerned,' he walked away hurriedly but was stopped midway by Gupta ji who appeared to be holding two different welcome kit samples.

After a brief word with his boss, Gupta ji walked up to me and said in a commanding voice, 'Gauri ji, tell your staff to remove the white welcome kits and put these brown folders instead.'

It was hilarious to note the sudden change in his tone, from the obsequious manner that he had used with Mr Mediratta to the authoritative one he was using with me now. Gupta ji added, 'And, hand over the white folders personally to me.

They have to be placed in the delegation rooms on the other floor. I am waiting right here since this matter is very urgent.'

At the same time, it was a relief to see the scores of special duty staff and security personnel finally evacuating the rooms as they herded themselves together near the guest elevators. I signalled my staff to start preparing the rooms immediately. Instead of working separately on different sections, they joined together to do a quick job on the entire floor. I decided not to interfere in their work plan. To save time, I went ahead to replace the welcome kits myself.

'Are you happy now that you have the custody of the rooms?' Mr Mediratta shouted from a distance. 'The rooms must look impeccable, just the way they were before the security checks. Please brief your staff accordingly.' He sounded as if he had done a huge favour to the hotel staff by handing over almost twenty ransacked rooms barely half an hour before the high-profile delegates were scheduled to arrive.

I was seething; nevertheless, I put up a fake smile and replied, 'We shall try our best, sir.'

Since the welcome kits were quite heavy, I got hold of a room service trolley and loaded it with twenty brown folders.

I observed that the brown folders were of low quality as compared to the white ones that had already been placed in the rooms. The white folders contained embedded calculators, ivory-finished carved pens, coloured documents in glossy papers, a small pack of mouth freshener, a high-quality notepad and some other stationery items. But the brown folders simply contained some black and white printouts with a very basic notepad and a pen.

'Why would anyone want to downgrade the level of welcome kits? There must have been some mistake,' I decided to check the matter once again with Gupta ji who was standing right beside me.

'Gupta ji, I hope there has been no mistake. The brown folders are not quite as nice as the white ones, you see,' I said while displaying both the folders to him. 'The white ones look so much better. Can't these be left in the rooms?'

'Gauri ji, you please do whatever has been told to you. I am aware about the quality of the welcome kits,' Gupta ji replied in a rather rude tone. He added, 'The higher quality welcome kits have been reserved for slightly senior delegates staying on another floor. This floor will be occupied only by junior delegates and therefore, the cheaper folders go here.'

I fully empathized with the junior delegates and prayed that this discrimination did not reflect badly on the hotel. Inevitably, the cocktail of brown and white folders would be discovered during the conference, signifying the different statuses.

By now, my spirits had dampened because of the response given by Gupta ji. I also kept wondering about the 'secret' criteria that would have been used to segregate 'junior' and 'senior' delegates. As far as we were concerned, the hotel staff, including the general manager and all the heads of the departments, had paid equal attention to both the elite floors; for us, they were identical in status. I suddenly felt sidelined for being incharge of the 'not-so-important' delegates.

Time was running out and there were still many rooms that had to be inspected. The staff had been working tirelessly in redoing the rooms and I chose to trail them and inspect the rooms. After working in close tandem with them for almost an hour, the last room was cleared just in time before the guest elevators rang.

The group of esteemed foreign delegates had finally arrived. We had been lucky; the guests had been delayed by forty-five minutes because of some demonstration outside. I couldn't thank those demonstrators enough. I don't know who they were—environmentalists, activists of bird rights, insect rights, human rights, gender rights, transgender rights, or gay rights—but, they had caused a huge traffic jam right outside the hotel. It had saved us from the embarrassment of making the delegates wait in the lobby as we cleaned their rooms.

A silent cheer was ringing all through the corridor. The delegates were absolutely thrilled with the ceremonial welcome of arti, teeka and garlands, an age old Indian custom of receiving guests respectfully. They were ushered into their respective rooms by well-groomed hotel executives who handed them their room keys. Representatives from the foreign embassy and the ministry also had made their presence felt during the welcoming greeting. However, Mr Mediratta was missing in action, at least on the 'not-so-important' eighth floor. Tonnes of luggage held together on neatly polished metallic trolleys got delivered to each room by a fleet of bell boys.

An hour later, the chaos finally subsided. The foreign embassy and the ministry representatives left. A few state policemen and security guards paced up and down the corridor while others rested on banquet chairs provided by the hotel. Not much action was expected till evening. All was quiet outside the rooms of the jet-lagged foreign delegates. Only a few crackling radio sounds were coming from hand-held security walkie-talkies interspersed with involuntary beeps coming out of the makeshift security gate, comforting the delegates that they were well-protected.

♦

27 February 2003 (The Crow's Justice)
It was half past eight in the morning.

After the complex security checks got over, the housekeeping staff had lined up their cleaning trolleys in the guest corridor of the eighth floor. Forty-five minutes had passed and they were still waiting for their work day to begin. Being the floor incharge, I had been asked to instruct the staff to not ring the doorbells to offer their cleaning services. The foreign delegates were expected to leave the floor at 9 a.m. for buffet breakfast and attend a half-day conference. Lunch was to be served at the picturesque open-air poolside in the warm winter sunshine. Thereafter, a visit to the landmark locations in the city had been planned to help them enjoy the rich cultural heritage of India.

After ninety minutes of agonizing wait, which had begun at 7.30 a.m., the delegates finally came out of their guest rooms at 9 a.m. They appeared in neat rows and took the guest elevators downstairs to the coffee shop for breakfast. No sooner had the delegates left than the floor housekeeping staff began servicing the guest rooms with full gusto.

I was relieved to watch the staff under my charge finally start their day of work.

However, the calmness was short-lived as I spotted several security guards walk up to the eighth-floor housekeeping staff and park themselves at the threshold of the guest rooms that were being cleaned.

'Gauri ma'am! Can you come here, please?' exclaimed one of the senior female room attendants. The sense of being watched upon by a guard was making her feel awkward. I walked up to her.

'Why is he here? Why is that machine gun pointed at me? And what pleasure does he seek in watching a fat cleaning lady like me who is almost his mother's age, do my daily work?' she griped, 'Look at their audacity! First these guys delay my work by two hours and then intrude upon my workspace. And, I am also sick of these repeated security checks done by boys who were not even born when I had joined this hotel!' she complained.

I tried to pacify her by helping her in making the bed. Soon, all other room attendants followed suit. After making all twenty beds with my team, I felt drained of all my energy. Then, I reminded myself that the delegates were scheduled to check out the next day. It was just a matter of a few more hours!

Still, it had been a hard day for everyone working on the eighth floor. Lunch was given a miss since a large number of rooms had to be serviced in a relatively short span of time. However, at the end of the morning shift, I accompanied the team down to the staff cafeteria for some tea and hot snacks.

We sat in the cafeteria holding hot cups of tea and several plates of samosas.[1] The canteen was buzzing with excitement. Sitting on our right was the banquet food service staff who had interesting stories to narrate about the poolside lunch that had been hosted for the foreign delegation.

I could also hear the name of Mr Hiten Mediratta being uttered every now and then. The arrogant look on the face of the young protocol officer was hard to miss by anyone, and the banquet captain and stewards were no exception. I decided to partake in their tale of encounters with the Indian bureaucracy. I thought it might make me feel better after a grinding day at work. Among other stories, I still remember this one episode which left all of us in disbelief and shock!

The lunch venue had been set up with utmost care and perfection at the quaint poolside. The pool tiles were sparkling clean and the garden landscape boasted of fresh

---

[1]Fried pastry with a savoury filling of spiced potatoes

seasonal flowers laid in multiple neat rows. Sweet chirping and occasional cawing echoed all around as a variety of birds played in the warm winter sun. Some of them pecked at the pool while others hunted for food on the vast stretches of green lawns. A few could also be seen hopping around garden sprinklers and fountains.

Chairs and circular tables were decorated with the highest quality of linen. The buffet food display was set up at a convenient distance from the sitting area. The chafing dishes had been lined up neatly with a few live cooking counters. The best silverware cutlery was polished and laid out, along with gold-embossed porcelain crockery. The glassware sparkled in the warm sunshine while some true vintage wines were stored on wine stands, often peeping out from those crushed ice buckets. The waiting staff, including stewards, hostesses and captains, wore their uniform in style and held clean white service cloths and aprons.

The theme was designed around yellow and white by choosing appropriate table and buffet counter linen. Circular flower arrangements consisting of yellow and white Dutch roses and green foliage were added to the tables, giving them a classy finished look. The food menu consisted of signature Indian dishes, notably daal makhani[2], naan[3], sarson ka saag[4] and butter chicken along with assorted Continental and Oriental cuisine. Although the luncheon had been planned as a sit-down meal with banquet stewards serving food, the foreign embassy representatives put forth a special request.

---

[2] Lentil curry cooked in Indian spices topped with loads of cream
[3] Indian bread cooked in charcoal grill
[4] Leaves of mustard, fenugreek and spinach cooked in Indian spices, served with dollops of butter

They wished to savour some live Indian cooking and wanted to serve themselves. Therefore, arrangements were done keeping in mind both aspects of food service. A welcome sign had been placed at the pool entrance coupled with a flower arrangement.

Mr Mediratta, along with his assistant, Gupta ji, had already inspected the banquet arrangements. Even the special security guards and state police personnel had approved the banquet site.

Meanwhile, Gupta ji had changed into some fresh clothes. There seemed to be an uncanny resemblance between him and the special duty canine squad members. To begin with, both salivated generously over the global cuisine, although the dogs had to retreat and make peace with their bowls of dog food. Next, both were on a leash. While the dogs wore their regular neck bands, Gupta ji struggled with his worn-out tie that must have been looped at least twenty years ago. Lastly, they both gave out a heady smell of mixed odours—sweat, food, cheap local scents and dried-up saliva.

A lot of back and forth had happened regarding the display text for the welcome board and the placement of name cards on the dining tables, especially those of the prime ministers. One could easily imagine what schemes were brewing in the minds of the special duty officers and other staff members. Could it be, 'Let me save the seat next to the prime minister for myself so I might be in the same frame as him in a photograph or two,' or maybe it was, 'Let me assign the seat next to mine to Ms Hawte from the foreign embassy. I have had my eyes on her for a long time and who knows we might manage to fix up a date together?'

Meanwhile, Gupta ji had done his bit of loud-mouthing with the food service staff. A complete list of dos and don'ts had been conveyed to the manager and other hotel staff. It mostly detailed the strict sequence of events that had to be followed during the formal luncheon. And, of course, he also asked the food service staff to address Mr Mediratta as 'sir' in the same brazen manner that had been experienced by me the day before. In good time, everyone seemed well-prepared to receive the esteemed delegates. Mr Mediratta placed himself at the welcome entrance to greet the guests. However, he stood away from the event hostess, lest his gracious presence get diluted amidst mere hoteliers.

Gupta ji had been sent away from the front line by his boss. Thus, he conveniently parked himself behind the buffet counters to drown his sorrows in the heavenly aroma and taste of the sumptuous food. One could spot him dipping his fingers in the starter section, licking them clean and rubbing the lingering remains of oils and spices on his palms like drops of hand moisturizer. A few special duty staff members and delegates also shook their hands with Gupta ji, blissfully unaware of the layers of saliva mixed with oils and spices left behind on their palms.

In due course, the luncheon took place as planned and in close alignment with the protocol. The prime ministers of both nations had already arrived for lunch after several fruitful rounds of discussions and agreements. The esteemed delegates also occupied their designated seats when the lunch was formally announced by the Master of Ceremonies. While food was being served at the prime ministers' table and that of a few others, most of the foreign delegates and embassy representatives started walking towards the buffet counter for self-service.

Gupta ji, who was still in his food-tasting spree behind the buffet counter, became slightly nervous at the sight of so many foreign eyes suddenly on him while his mouth was still stuffed with half-chewed food. By now, the food service staff, stationed beside him, had become disgusted with his continuous nagging and constant advice related to the quality of food and service. The uniformed staff would have done anything to get rid of his parasitic presence.

But there was a bigger disaster waiting!

Just as the delegates took their first hungry steps towards the buffet counter, one of the crows perched above decided to drop its excrement right into the daal makhani chafing dishes. The banquet steward standing behind the chafing dish noticed the bird poop despite the rich brownish-black lentils camouflaging it. He watched the crow helplessly as it carried on with its usual cawing thereafter!

The banquet steward started waving his arms and whistling out to his senior in an act of extreme desperation while wanting to remove the dish right away. In between, he also continued smiling at the fast-approaching delegates to cover up the mishap. The neighbouring steward nudged his shoulder and frowned at him for his atrocious and untimely act of jugglery. He reminded the former of the detailed lecture-cum-demonstration given on the correct behaviour by the senior captain steward and Gupta ji just before the luncheon began. His senior also shushed him from a distance pointing at the glaring eyes of Mr Mediratta. Also, Gupta ji held his saliva and spice smeared index finger over his lips like a kindergarten teacher asking the banquet steward to stay quiet and resume composure.

By then, the delegates had already reached the buffet counter and had started serving themselves the food from the salad section. At first, the steward merely looked on as he couldn't have fished anything out from the dish in front of the consistent stare of guests. So, he did the best possible thing under the circumstances. He picked up the service gear and stirred the lentil curry well to spread out the bird dropping uniformly as the high concentration of crow excrement in one morsel of daal makhani might have been fatal for the unlucky person who would have served himself *that* part of the lentil curry.

The other stewards and guests accepted it, without question, as a harmless and usual service practice. Nobody guessed the pressing need behind this final stir except for Gupta ji who had grown suspicious by now.

He grimaced and asked cynically, 'Why did you stir the daal makhani in such a tearing hurry, young boy?'

The steward replied promptly, 'To enhance its flavour by mixing the cream well into the spiced lentils. This is a standard procedure we follow here, Gupta ji.'

Even though he was not fully convinced by the steward's response, Gupta ji had to leave in a hurry as he had been summoned by his boss. Mr Mediratta appeared rather displeased with the food devouring ways of Gupta ji and decided to distract his attention towards some tasks away from the buffet counters.

As a result, Gupta ji was nowhere to be seen for the next couple of hours!

The foreign delegates were thrilled with the quality of food and service. Daal makhani, especially, was a big hit among the guests as they took second and third helpings of the hot lentil curry and ate it with fresh warm naan, coming right out of the live charcoal grill in the winter afternoon.

The prime ministers were also appreciative of the wonderful lentil curry.

Thereafter, the luncheon was largely uneventful. After the hearty meal, the foreign delegates and embassy representatives went ahead with their city sightseeing as scheduled. Luxury tourist buses had already lined up at the hotel porch waiting for the sightseers. Mr Mediratta also left along with the esteemed guests, completely unaware of the daal makhani mishap or, rather, mix-up!

'Phew!' exclaimed the banquet steward after narrating the story of the 'special' daal makhani to us in the cafeteria.

'So, you see, that was so close! What else could I do? Everybody around me shushed me. And Gupta ji almost threatened me with closed fists. I made sure that he was served some extra portions of the lentil curry after his return towards the end of the luncheon. Divine justice was served. Hail the crow! Long live the crow!'

I was too dumbfounded to react to the story. Although even the housekeeping staff of the eighth floor had wished for some form of revenge, this crow's justice was way too exaggerated for us. And we had never meant for any harm to befall the unassuming foreign delegates.

By the time the story came to an end, tea cups were lying empty and samosa plates had been licked clean. It was late as we all walked out of the cafeteria after a long day of work and gossip. On my way out, I caught a glimpse of the dinner menu being written on the white board of the staff canteen. The names of the dishes had been neatly written as per the courses.

And one of them was daal makhani!

FACE OF A MOB

'Can you hear us? Please nod if you can hear us.'

Faint voices rang in my ears as I struggled to open my eyes. My hands and feet felt like they had been tied together. Many wires lay spread across my body. An irritating beeping sound played relentlessly in the background. Cold hands kept shaking my body mercilessly to bring me out of restful spells.

Perhaps I had slept for too long.

But where was I? Why didn't my body react to my mental commands? How I wished to open my eyes and move my limbs but I couldn't. I tried harder...and harder...and harder!

There!

I finally managed to open my eyes just a little bit. Two nurses and a doctor were staring back at me, their gaze alternating between the health monitors and my body.

Had I been lying on a hospital bed all this while? What had happened to me? The last thing I could remember was crossing the road and an auto rickshaw zooming towards me. Was it last evening when I had been returning home from work? The doctor guessed that I felt a bit lost. He explained the situation to me.

'Don't worry, Gauri. You are better now. Last evening you were brought here unconscious after being hit by a speeding vehicle. We placed you under observation and initiated the first line of treatment. Your condition has stabilized faster than we had anticipated. But you still need to stay here for at least another two days.'

'I want to speak with my parents.' These words sprang out from my parched lips instantly.

'Don't worry, they have already been informed. In fact, they will be here with you in just a couple of hours. Many of your colleagues were here this morning to visit you and complete the hospital formalities. Most of them have left, except a few. You can meet them if you want,' the doctor replied and pointed towards the open blinds of my room's window.

I looked out of the glass to find some familiar faces from the hotel.

Hell! Of all the seventy-odd staff members from the housekeeping department, the two men I hated most stood there—Laloo and Mukesh Dandekar.

'Would you like to meet them?' The doctor interrupted my thoughts.

'No, thank you. I am fine,' I responded.

After a few more routine check-ups, the doctor prepared to leave along with his team of nurses. 'Just press the button beside your bed if you wish to contact us. We'll be back after lunch. Take care till then,' he said and closed the door behind him.

I was left alone in the room, unable to move, an intravenous drip and finger sensor stuck to my body. With nothing much to do, I continued staring out of the glass window. There was a lot of movement in the hospital corridor. And Laloo and Mukesh Dandekar still stood there.

I could not stop myself from thinking about both of them and how much I disliked them!

◆

Laloo, a 'sorry' token of spoken English

'I come after you to check room.'

'No, Laloo, that's not how it is said. Please repeat the correct phrase after me. "I shall come back to your room and fix the problem later".'

'I fix you later in the room.'

'Again, Laloo, it's wrong. You are not paying complete attention to what I am saying, are you?'

I was about to lash out at Laloo further, during a spoken English class, but better sense prevailed and I quickly resumed my display of fake pleasantness. Nevertheless, it was getting increasingly difficult to hold back my growing impatience. At least a dozen teaching sessions must have gone by without fruition. Laloo had failed to utter a single English phrase correctly. Or, perhaps, I had failed to teach him.

It was an unusual situation! Laloo wasn't the quintessential keen young learner. And I wasn't a qualified language instructor, nor had I ever desired to become one. I was no educator or academician but a mere housekeeping manager. But now, both of us were being forced to sit together in the linen room, often hidden away from the prying eyes of the hotel staff, so I could help Laloo learn some basic stuff in spoken English. The teaching content had been earnestly titled 'Standard English Phrases in Hotel Housekeeping'. But, if truth be told, I felt quite burdened with this added responsibility that stifled my already tight work schedule.

While I had to stay back after my duty hours to teach him, Laloo was privileged enough to attend learning sessions during his work shift. There was perfect synchronicity between my diction and his actions; while I delved into prepositions, he would reposition his sluggish body and mind, and with his thumb and index fingers, he would explore the tunnels of his hairy nostrils and would only bounce back to alertness on finding a few dried remains of nasal mucus. Rest of the time, his droopy eyes would stare blankly at me.

Once, he smirked and said, 'Madam ji, I can't learn English this way. Why don't you just give me a sheet of phrases in Hindi? And don't forget to add a small sketch beside each phrase as a learning cue, you know, like a glass of water or a clock. It might help me in using the phrases with the guests correctly.'

I glared at him in silence, shocked by his audacity to belittle my teaching attempts despite my busy work schedule.

'So, Madam ji, may I leave for the day? It is already five minutes past four. My duty has already ended. When shall we meet next?'

'Next Monday,' I replied.

'Okay, Madamji. And I hope that you would be ready with the English phrases in Hindi with supporting pictures for the next class,' Laloo reminded me in a brazen manner and left the linen room.

Actually, he had special immunity that protected him against any disciplinary or corrective action. He was the brother-in-law of the vice president of the employees' trade union. Apart from this incidental qualification, he did not hold any other merit.

I felt thorough disillusionment when I faced the real side of worker unions. The truth was in complete contrast to the philosophy behind The Indian Trade Unions Act, 1926 and labour bureau guidelines which seem as bogus theories taught during management training.

In reality, trade unions were *voluntary* organizations causing *involuntary* mess at the hotel workplace. Years ago, what must have begun as a torch-bearing entity of worker interests and welfare, was now reduced to an unruly 'mob' with a bunch of selfish individuals seeking cheap favours for themselves and their sycophants. The collective bargaining power that was supposed to improve service conditions and wages for workers seemed to have been reduced to fictitious disputes between hotel management and union leaders just to please helpless workers with less educated background.

While genuine demands, such as quality of staff meals, medical facilities, staff lockers, training and development got voiced occasionally, the union leaders mostly threw their weight around to covert bargains, such as getting better performance ratings assigned to chosen workers, closing genuine disciplinary actions against close employees and discount the long breaks and on-duty disappearances of certain 'chosen' workers. Even the slightest change in work descriptions had to be negotiated with union leaders. These issues were discussed openly but never recorded.

Like everywhere else, in hotels too, trade unions became divided along political lines. This had led to the creation of multiple unions in one hotel, thereby fragmenting the collective bargaining power of the workers—an intelligent move to tame the crowd. So what if a few complimentary meals were doled out to political representatives, at least the workers could be kept suppressed.

Laloo was just another worker fancied by the worker union. He had been employed as a floor polisher in the housekeeping department. One could easily spot him taking undue breaks during duty hours. He also returned at least an hour late from lunch every day. His large and lethargic body had long been addicted to frequent rounds of stolen meals and rest.

It was easy to spot him from behind. He had droopy shoulders and his huge buttocks were hard to accommodate inside a standard set of the white uniform dungarees. The front was no different either! He scratched his crotch quite often as a result of an ever-growing paunch pulling the dungaree pants upwards. The employees in charge of the uniforms were forced to let out the waist of his dungarees every six months to make room for his ever-growing abdominal area. His dark and obese body gave out a mixed pungent odour of fermented sweat and chewed gutka.[5]

On the rare occasions that he did work, his breath would become unsteady, forcing him to take frequent gasps of air while talking. Apart from the breath issue, he also suffered, quite often, from flatulence, especially upon squatting. His huge bottom invariably held large amounts of trapped gases owing to his erratic eating and resting habits.

Laloo had stunted and impaired cognitive abilities. He was slow to understand, react and follow instructions. It was hard to say whether it stemmed from a genuine genetic disorder or his visible lack of interest at work. His peers often pointed out that he couldn't even comprehend humour during the staff canteen jokes. But, if stuck under unfavourable situations, he was alert enough to cite his powerful association with the trade union vice president. Needless to say, it was no less than a nightmare to monitor his work as an area manager.

Both of us clearly hated each other because Laloo and I had been involved in a couple of spoken English debacles concerning hotel guests. It was just by sheer chance that I was his area manager on both the occasions.

---

[5] Addictive preparation of crushed areca nut, tobacco, catechu, paraffin wax, slaked lime and sweet or savoury flavourings

The first incident had occurred at the poolside on a cold winter morning. Since resident guests refrained from using the outdoor pool during winters, it was under-repair for thorough tile cleaning. The water had been drained out for cleaning the floor tiles and repairing the walls.

Laloo was using a steam machine to clean the grooves in the bordering tiles and had forgotten to place the 'pool under repair' signage at the pool's entrance. Other sets of signage such as 'no diving', 'shallow waters', 'caution—wet floor', etc. had also been removed.

Just then, a daring Norwegian gentleman made an unguarded entry into the pool area. Scandinavian guests never took the tropical winters too seriously! It was common to spot them in just a full-sleeved shirt and trousers when the hotel staff would be wrapped up in layers of warm clothing. Some of them even stepped out in shorts and a t-shirt during chilly informal evenings.

It was quite early in the morning when this winter-resistant gentleman struggled to find his way around the pool that was covered in a wintery haze. He was slightly old and also seemed to have weak vision.

Coping with his minimal sight, he somehow located the sunbathing beds and poolside umbrellas. He chose one bed to store his towel, a pair of slippers, and suntan lotion along with some books and his reading glasses. Satisfied with himself on being an early bird to visit the poolside, he removed the towelling bathrobe that he wore. Walking up to the edge of the pool towards the diving board, he spotted Laloo working at a distance.

'Hi there! Is it ok if I take a dive here?' he asked waving his hands at him.

Laloo felt a little perturbed at being summoned by the

half-naked guest. He turned behind him to see if anyone else was around. Then, true to his traits, he did not bother answering. Also, it is safe to assume, he couldn't understand what the gentleman was asking. Whatever the case may have been, Laloo decided not to involve himself in a conversation with the guest.

Meanwhile, the elderly gentleman mistook Laloo's silence for an agreeing nod and began to get ready for the plunge into the empty pool, which was still covered with a light wintery haze. He circled his arms to warm up and also did a few sit-ups. Like a skilful deepwater diver, he bent his body forward and...

Disaster struck!

The gentleman crashed into the empty pool. Badly hurt and bleeding, he began yelling for help.

Finally, Laloo rushed to the pool. He realized then what the guest had meant to ask him a couple of minutes back. But it was too late! Knowing that the delicate pool stairs will not be able to sustain his heavy body, he rushed inside to get more help. Being the area manager, I was also summoned at the poolside. Meanwhile, the arrangements for an ambulance and stretcher were also made. Dr Nigam was also alerted.

A rescue operation ensued with the help of ropes, hardboard, two double bed sheets and a team of six agile hotel staff members. After almost half an hour of intense team work, the elderly guest could be pulled out safely from the empty pool. He was rushed to the nearest hospital with Dr Nigam by his side.

Quite understandably, the guest had been seriously wounded. There were multiple fractures and a severe head injury. Months of medical treatment were required before the elderly gentleman could fly back to his home country.

Meanwhile, the hotel went through a horrible ordeal of

managing legal threats, news reporters and diplomatic perils from the Norwegian embassy along with bearing the costs of providing free air tickets and complimentary hotel stay for the family members of the injured guest.

Anticipating that some form of action could be taken against him, Laloo had already approached the worker union. The trade union vice president tried his best to protect his sister's husband from being punished. All arguments were based on his lack of spoken English knowledge. Laloo was being projected as a helpless worker who could continue to prove himself as a worthy asset to the hotel, just with a little assistance from the hotel in teaching him spoken English. It was also termed wrong to shame a worker only because he wasn't privileged enough to receive a formal education in his childhood.

As for me, I left no stone unturned in reaffirming my perspective on the negligence of duty displayed by Laloo. It wasn't just about spoken English! It was about being vigilant and ensuring timely placement of poolside signage. It was about the will to walk up to the guest. It was about making an extra effort to fetch help from English-speaking staff members. It wasn't very difficult to convince the bosses that Laloo had been negligent on duty.

Nevertheless, it was a completely different matter when it came to what action could be taken against him. Behind closed doors, the trade union decided to threaten the management. The office bearers and working committee members tried to intimidate the executive council with dire consequences during the negotiation of charter of demands, which was just around the corner.

Finally, Laloo resumed work after being given just a mild warning to be more careful and seek help from other team members, if faced with a similar situation. He flashed a victorious smile as he walked past me at the housekeeping office. I quietly turned my face away. My boss asked me to prepare a crash course in spoken English tailored to the learning needs of Laloo.

However, I kept delaying the teaching task with the hope that the poolside accident would soon be forgotten by all.

But it was not to be!

Just weeks later, Laloo managed to create yet another stir. This time, the hotel had to bear far more profound consequences than the previous occasion.

A certain Ms Valarie Benton was visiting the hotel on behalf of a reputed global hotel chain, Six Seasons. She was the director-partnerships and an important decision maker. She always seemed to dress impeccably, mostly in sleek business skirt suits. The soft wrinkles on her pale white face were often concealed under layers of make up, smoky eye shadows and cherry-red lipsticks. It was enriching to interact with her since she gave out a wonderful sense of wisdom and experience, perhaps owing to her long and glorious career, spanning over three decades in the business.

Her visit marked the first round of talks on the feasibility of co-branding between both the hotel chains. It meant more visibility, increased international business and rise in hospitality ranking for the hotel where I worked. She was accompanied by a team of four, two hotel process auditors and two co-branding experts.

That afternoon, Ms Benton decided to explore the hotel spa and wellness centre, all by herself. There had been several rounds of fruitful discussions over the previous three days and her team had many good things to report back about our hotel. However, she seemed to have grown a bit bored of all the constant attention and foreign company, and desired some rest and solitude.

She found the elevator landing to the wellness centre understandably quiet, with incense sticks burning in one corner. In the background of soft lighting and chimes of Oriental tunes, she began to admire the intricate gold patchwork on the high-rise walls.

And then, she saw Laloo standing beside the hydraulic ladder with piles of dusters and cleaning sprays. He had been paired up with one of the smarter workers to do the high level dusting and spotlight cleaning. Laloo had been instructed to simply operate the hydraulic ladder and help his partner scale up and down the walls. He felt proud and capable, stationed beside the interesting red piece of machinery. It was made up of several folding arms and criss-cross rod sections which contracted and expanded when closed and opened.

Ms Benton approached the hydraulic ladder with admiration. Since his partner was away to close down a section of lights for cleaning, Laloo was left behind to face the guest single-handedly. He felt a little nervous in front of the sophisticated Ms Benton. Till then, the only two English words Laloo could speak and understand confidently were 'yes' and 'no' apart from a few general greetings.

In an adventurous spirit, Ms Benton decided to climb up the hydraulic ladder platform. Laloo also extended full support and helped her get onto the lattice platform with a metal railing support. He secured her inside by closing shut all the latches from outside. So far so good, thought Ms Benton and got bolder.

'Can I go just a little higher? I want to know how it feels to move up and down,' she tried to explain to Laloo with her hands raised up.

Immediately, Laloo pressed the 'move up' green button as hard as he could.

Zoom!

In just a few seconds, Ms Benton reached the highest point with her head almost touching the ceiling of the high-rise wall.

Meanwhile, Laloo's cleaning partner was still grappling with the electrical circuit board and had accidentally turned off the power to the hydraulic ladder.

Ms Benton could never imagine that her simple request of moving up a few inches would be met with such fierce and prompt fervour. She began to panic and scream, realizing that the machine operator could not understand her language. Laloo also began sweating nervously for not being able to figure out why the machine had stopped working.

All his attempts to make eye contact and pacify Ms Benton provoked her further because the contact that Laloo was trying to make with her eyes inadvertently landed on her panties! Yes, the platform floor was see-through owing to its metallic mesh finish.

Amid all the chaos, Laloo could not help smirking each time Ms Benton screamed while attempting to pull her skirt together and save her modesty from getting outraged. Hearing all the noise and commotion, staff members began to arrive by dozens around the hydraulic ladder, only to see the pink satin panties worn by Ms Benton.

Almost fifteen minutes later, the power to the hydraulic ladder was restored and Ms Benton was brought down safely. Her face had turned red as she kept shivering from nervousness and embarrassment.

'I beg your pardon!' she whispered, wiping away the tears on her face as she made her way through the crowd and rushed to catch the elevator back to her room.

Needless to say, the prestigious co-branding aspirations of the hotel with Six Seasons had been chucked away along with the pink satin panties worn by the respectable director, who then stuck to wearing trousers till the day of her departure.

And yet again, Laloo could not be tried under any disciplinary action owing to the punitive immunity that he enjoyed. On the contrary, I was reprimanded for delaying the spoken English classes that were meant to enrich him.

Now began my struggle to create those special handouts consisting of transcripts and drawings.

I often thought, 'When will Laloo finally learn to speak English?'

Mukesh Dandekar at the W.C. Training

'Key card lockout! Key card lockout! Key card lockout!'

'Management, stay warned! Management, stay warned! Management, stay warned!'

'Key card lockout! Key card lockout! Key card lockout!'

I was welcomed by a group of at least three dozen workers that morning, protesting against the management. The important members of the trade union working committee stood there in full attendance. It was seven in the morning when duties had to be allocated and keys handed over.

None of the department heads were present in the hotel. They were expected to take charge only two hours later. However, the front desk was in urgent need of clean rooms to accommodate early morning check-ins, public areas such as toilets, elevators and restaurants had to be cleaned, and the housekeeping desk was flooded with guest requests of extra shoeshine and towels, soaps, ironing and room cleaning.

Actually, the trouble had begun the previous day when

a theft had been reported by a guest staying on the third floor. Mukesh Dandekar, a senior room attendant who had cleaned the guest room, had been questioned by the police over the reportedly missing items. Mukesh happened to be part of the trade union working committee. He also enjoyed certain political affiliations.

All hell broke loose after the police interrogation got over. The missing items had been found by the guest who subsequently sent out gracious and heartfelt apologies to all the concerned hotel staff. But Mukesh had been left humiliated in front of the guest and junior staff members. He planned the protest against the management for allowing uninhibited access to the police into questioning a staff member of his stature.

Consequently, the workers refused to clean rooms unless the area managers took charge of the keys and accompanied them when they cleaned the guest rooms. However, the expectation was almost impossible to fulfil, given the expanse of area each manager had been given to supervise.

I handed over the desk calls to two junior housekeeping managers while I called my boss, Ms Malini Pande at her residence. It was important to apprise her on the staff protest and take her advice regarding the next steps.

Ms Pande was a seasoned executive housekeeper having a long work association with the company. She had begun her career as a laundry supervisor almost twenty-seven years back and now was the director—accommodation services. Known to be extremely dedicated to her job, she never married nor stayed with her family. The work standards set by her were difficult to achieve by most people.

But she wasn't very popular among the hotel staff. Ms Pande held strong views on matters and had biased opinions about people. She often lacked concern for the familial duties of married staff members who had children to look after.

'Good morning, ma'am. This is Gauri.'

'Good morning?' Ms Pande replied in a puzzled and broken voice.

'I'm sorry for disturbing you, ma'am, but there is a massive staff protest happening right now. The workers refuse to sign for their keys. Front desk is asking for clean rooms, guest requests are pouring in and lobby cloak rooms are lying dirty. I need your advice,' I replied, almost out of breath.

'Calm down, Gauri! Everything will be sorted out. Now, tell me how many managers are there on duty?'

'We are five managers in total. Two of us are junior and relatively new here.'

'Alright then, send the junior managers to the public areas. They can also run a few errands for you. The senior managers can go to the guest rooms. Meanwhile, you handle the desk and guest calls.'

'Ok ma'am. The managers will reach their locations as advised by you. And then?'

'And then what, Gauri?'

'I mean what would they be doing?'

'They would be cleaning the public areas and guest rooms, of course! What else did you think?'

'Uh-huh! Fine, ma'am,' I replied, still trying to believe what I had just heard from my boss—managers assigned with the task of workers.

'We shall try to sort out the matter by evening today. Also inform the evening and night shift managers to report on duty three hours early. It won't be possible for just five managers to clean so many rooms and public areas.'

'Ok, ma'am.'

'I will try and reach the office in another hour. Will you be able to manage by then?'

'Don't worry, ma'am. We shall try our best.'

The phone had been disconnected. I was finding it difficult to break the news of Ms Pande's work plan to my peers. The bluntness in her voice was hard to forget. We, as managers, were not even given the opportunity to graciously volunteer to clean rooms and public toilets. Rather, it was being forced as a natural expectation.

Nevertheless, the new plan was shared quickly since there was no time to complain! In a matter of a few minutes, the managers left for their areas.

I quickly took over the housekeeping desk while the slogans and protests still continued outside the housekeeping department. The general manager had already called for a morning meeting between the executive council and the trade union general council to resolve the issue at the earliest.

But the rest of the day was extremely tense for everyone.

By afternoon, all the workers had left the hotel premises. There wasn't much for them to do at the hotel anyway.

But the 'manager-workers' kept giving me constant updates about the tough task that lay ahead of them. The lobby and banquet toilets had been ravaged the night before by crowds of wedding guests. The cloak rooms were filled with the stink of alcohol puke and ammonia from dried urine. The wedding guests had departed leaving behind scores of ridiculously dirty rooms. It was an uphill task for the managers to get all the areas back into order.

Yet, they held the front as true soldiers, never failing to share warm smiles with the guests, and not letting go of their polite mannerisms despite the hostile conditions.

A few industrial trainees from the nearby hotel management

institutes and some contractual window cleaners also helped in cleaning the hotel.

Meanwhile, the closed door meeting carried on in full swing. The general manager presided over the talks between the executive council and trade union general council. The only news that reached us was their tea, coffee and meal orders, and nothing else.

Finally, the meeting ended.

It had gone on till late evening. Dinner with drinks was being arranged at the best hotel suite for the group of twenty-odd members, belonging to both the trade union general council and executive council.

Later that night, Ms Pande walked into the department to meet all of us. Perhaps she wished to boost our morale and thank us for working hard to guard the honour and reputation of the hotel.

'How was the meeting, ma'am?' I asked eagerly. The other managers also joined the conversation.

'Well! There's some good news. But first of all I would like to thank all of you for the wonderful show today. It was excellent team work. Hip-hip hurrah! Hip-hip hurrah! Hip-hip hurrah!' Ms Pande seemed to be in high spirits.

The rest of us were standing like worn-out soldiers trying to save the last drops of feeble energy to travel back home. As much as we wished to join the cheer, there were only a few of us with smiles on our tired faces.

'So, the worker strike has been called off?' I asked full of hope.

'Yes. And there's more! The trade union working committee has agreed to undergo a specialized leadership development programme. It will help committee members like Mukesh Dandekar redefine their priorities whilst managing conflicts better. You know, most of these union members have never been privileged enough to get decent education and exposure. Therefore, such instances bring out the dark ignorance in them. Easy access to political networks further clouds their judgement. They lack the acumen that leaders have to be able to rise above the "self" to tackle difficult situations.'

Ms Pande could have lectured us the whole night since she was visibly high on sugar from so many rounds of tea and coffee. The profound phrases that she used seemed to be borrowed from her seniors at the meeting.

'What leadership development programme, ma'am?' I asked.

'The W.C. Training Programme where W.C. stands for Working Committee. It will be a three-day residential workshop at a farmhouse away from the main city. The programme begins day after tomorrow,' Ms Pande answered with fervour.

We managers just wished our painful day would end. Not only were our bodies tired, but our egos had been bruised too!

It was almost eleven in the night. Handing over the charge to the night shift supervisor and staff, we left the hotel. Ms Pande had also left by then.

The next day, everything returned to normal. Workers who had been forced to join the lockout came back to perform their usual duties. Junior supervisors also cooperated with the managers. The bitter incident had been forgotten, or so we tried to portray.

Then weeks later, I happened to ask Mukesh Dandekar about his experience at the W.C. Training Programme.

'So, how was it? That leadership development programme you attended?' I enquired casually.

'Fantastic!' he winked back, with a mysterious smile.

Given the strange reaction, I was curious to ask more. 'Who

were the trainers? And did you get any learning material?'

He chuckled and replied, 'You really want to know about it? Well, we had dozens of fleshy voluptuous young girls as our trainers and endless crates of booze as our learning material!'

His loud audacious laughter kept reverberating through the hotel corridor.

◆

Back at the hospital, these painful reminders had kept me occupied. Laloo and Mukesh who stood right outside the cabin were completely unaware of the hateful glares that I directed at them from behind the glass.

I began to feel tired and anxious by then. Perhaps it was the hospital environment. I decided to close my eyes but I kept thinking about how mid-level managers like me were mere pawns squeezed between nepotism, greed and exploitation. As the executive council savoured day-long discussions over tea and coffee and the worker union representatives continued to enjoy 'residential training programmes', managers like us ended up cleaning the hotel by working double shifts.

Amid the claustrophobic walls of the hospital and my own haunting thoughts, I probably slept for a while.

'How are you feeling, my dear?' My mother hugged me tight as my father placed their luggage on the hospital room's floor.

A wave of relief washed over me as I finally saw my parents. I just held both of them close to me and wept for a long time.

Sometime later, the doctor arrived and had a detailed discussion with my father, while my mother sat beside me.

Almost half an hour later, the doctor left again.

'Who exactly informed you about my accident? Was it someone from the hotel?' I asked my father.

'Someone called Mukesh Dandekar. God bless him and his friend Laloo,' my father replied in an emotional voice and then continued on a different note, 'Curse these big metro towns. How can the crowds here mutely watch a helpless and unconscious young girl lying injured on the road? Don't they have daughters of their own? Not a single person came forward to help you!'

My mother added, 'Had it not been for those two angels, my daughter would have been as good as dead by now!' She tried to control her tears.

'Do you mean these two men here?' I pointed at Mukesh and Laloo still standing outside the window.

My mother smiled a little and confirmed, 'Yes, indeed my dear. I meant these very two men. What is the matter! Don't you remember your own hotel workers?'

'Spare her for the time being. The accident might have impacted some portions of her brain!' my father said laughing.

Suddenly, I turned quiet, trying to mentally process this surprising piece of information.

These two dreadfully hated men were my saviours!

I looked outside my window one more time to catch a glimpse of Laloo and Mukesh, who rested on metallic joined chairs. They were deep in conversation.

Had I missed something? Mukesh seemed so different today. A far cry from the hateful slogans he called out during the lockout, while Laloo had a concerned look on his otherwise blank face. Had I been too reckless in judging them? Were those fine human qualities in them overshadowed by the mob mentality of worker unions on previous occasions? They were persons in their own right, with a very small part of them belonging to the worker union.

A little while later, I expressed my new-found desire to

meet both of them. My father readily complied with my wish and ushered them into my room.

'Thank you, Laloo and Mukesh,' I was a little inhibited while resting on the hospital bed. 'My parents and I can't thank you enough for what you did last evening.'

'Don't bother, Gauri ma'am. While leaving from work last evening, we spotted you outside the hotel bus stop. You were lying unconscious on the road. We could have never left you alone in that terrible situation,' Mukesh spoke on behalf of Laloo as well.

'Get well soon, Gauri ma'am, we have to resume those English classes,' Laloo gave me a knowing smile.

I felt so safe and comfortable in that moment. I had my parents beside me with their unconditional parental love. But what made it more special was the accidental discovery of hidden affection in the eyes of two supposed adversaries.

As their small talk lulled my tired body into yet another spell of slumber, I wondered secretly—how can an individual face be so different from the face of its mob?

... THEN, A 'MELLOWED MANAGER'

Gauri alternates between the roles of a housekeeping manager and a home manager. She has her plate full! So much to do—help the boss run a complete department, resolve guest complaints, attend to new friends and relatives, buy groceries and cook meals.

Gauri does not even have time to complain! She gets more appreciative of the love, trust and faith shown by her hotel's staff and colleagues. She has earned it over the years by showing unwavering care and concern towards them. Guests do not seem daunting anymore. She savours wholehearted discussions with them.

Gauri recounts a few more experiences...

DID EYE LIE?

It was very cold.
It was almost two in the morning and the chilly winter breeze had frozen my face and lips into numbness. My head was wrapped in a woollen muffler. I had stuffed my hands into the pockets of my beige overcoat. The hotel uniform silk sari, which I wore over a cotton petticoat, concealed my woollen leggings. The pleats of my sari kept flapping like boat sails around my legs every now and then, making it difficult to walk. My toes also felt numb beneath two layers of socks. I had forced my feet into the uniform shoes, actually a pair of black leather kitten heels that protested against the increased dimensions of my foot as I struggled to place my steps firmly on the stone pavement during the inspection round of the hotel driveway.

In the dead silence, my only talking companion was the hand-held walkie-talkie which gave out frequent crackling sounds of nonchalant staff voices. The routine messages—that the banquet halls had been cleaned; the scrubbing of the hotel lobby floor had begun; the hotel key count had been tallied successfully by security; the telephone operator had continued on a double shift since the night shift person had called in sick; all female staff members from the evening shift had been dropped off safely; the computer systems had been shut down for the night audit; the boilers had been rested for four hours to save costs; and the night shift staff count was fifty—confirmed that all was well in the hotel!

Being the overall incharge of the hotel, I felt relieved to hear these messages. As much as I relished the night-long autonomy offered to me as the duty manager, it was also daunting to be accountable for anything and everything that could happen at the hotel. Right then, it was a property with two hundred and fifty rooms and over four hundred guests were sleeping inside peacefully, after entrusting their lives and belongings into the hands of just fifty-odd hotel staff members. But I tried not to dwell over this disturbing thought too much. Instead, it was more appealing for me to admire the quiet moments of work and sovereignty, something that I missed during the day amid full attendance of departmental heads and worker union leaders.

It was comforting to return to the warmth of the hotel lobby after the chilly inspection round of the hotel driveway and porch. I had barely removed my overcoat and woollen socks when the panic-stricken voice of the telephone operator crackled on my walkie-talkie.

'This is Stella from telephones. Gauri ma'am, please come in. This is very urgent! Gauri ma'am, please come in, over.'

I responded at once, 'This is Gauri here. I repeat, this is Gauri. Stella, please come in, over.'

'Gauri ma'am, please identify your location. I need to call you on a phone, over.'

'Please call the bell desk, over.'

'Gauri ma'am, please pick up the phone at the bell desk, over and out.'

The walkie-talkie went out as the bell desk phone rang in an instant. I had hardly picked up the receiver when Stella started talking in a high-pitched nervous voice, 'Thanks for answering the phone fast, Gauri ma'am. Actually, I am concerned about the guest in Room 1408. At this hour, he insists on meeting the general manager of the hotel in his room.'

'Why should any guest want to meet the general manager at 2:30 am? Did you ask him if he needs anything? Or whether he is feeling well or not?' I asked.

'I tried offering him several options, but he refused all of them blatantly. He has been holding on to the phone receiver for the last fifteen minutes. I still have him on the other line. He will not disconnect unless the general manager reaches his room,' Stella replied.

'Do you think it will be a good idea to talk to him over the phone?'

'Gauri ma'am, he doesn't talk, he only screams. It will be no use trying to reason with him about anything.'

I paused for a few seconds and said, 'Fine. I shall visit him right away in his room. Let's not disturb the GM just yet. I would like to first find out what he really wants. Give me his name and the company he works for. Is this his first visit to our hotel?' I held a pencil poised over a notepad.

Stella answered, reading from the computer records, 'He is Mr Solomon John, CEO of a shipping company in Kerala. This is his fifth visit to our hotel and all his previous visits have been uneventful. Based on passport details, he should be around forty-four years old.'

'Thanks, Stella. Just hold him on the line for another minute. I am starting for his room now. And, please ask one of the guest floor security staff members to reach the fourteenth floor and wait for me there. I really don't wish to challenge the privacy of a respectable gentleman in the middle of the night, all alone,' I said and added, 'He may have just woken up from a bad dream. If need be, we can also have Dr Nigam come over to examine him. But we can do that later.'

The phone disconnected as I tore off the scribbled page from the notepad and hurried to the guest floor. Suddenly, the cold left my body and I could feel drops of sweat oozing from my forehead and neck. The woollen leggings almost strangled me. I loosened the topmost button of my uniform blouse to feel a little better.

I memorized the name of the guest and struggled to create a sort of mental image of a man in his mid-forties, who headed the operations of a shipping company, and at present, chose to throw a childish tantrum in the middle of the night, among people he hardly knew on a personal level. What could have compelled him to summon the general manager at this hour on a freezing winter night? I looked around for the security staff member as I ascended to the fourteenth floor and felt relieved to see him standing right outside the door of Room 1408.

The security guard informed me that he had found the door of the room wide open when he had reached. Surprisingly, there was no sound coming from inside but all the room lights, including the bathroom lights, were switched on. The door of the room was open. I told the guard to knock briefly at the door and politely inform Mr John that the duty manager was here to meet him and that she was waiting outside the room.

As instructed, the security guard knocked at the door thrice, but got no response. He then identified himself loudly for the guest and walked into the room. There was a brief whispered exchange between the guard and the room occupant. Minutes later, the security guard came out perplexed and informed me that Mr John wanted to meet me at once. And he also assured me that the guest seemed decent enough to be able to converse with a lady.

I asked the security guard to remain outside the door unless instructed otherwise. It was important for me to have someone wait at the door for me till I came out of the room. Brushing aside my slight nervousness, I finally entered the room.

I announced my arrival in a soft voice, 'Good morning, Mr John. My name is Gauri and I am the duty manager.'

I took slow careful steps inside.

There he was! I could now clearly see Mr John crouched on the single sofa clasping the telephone receiver with both his hands. Perhaps Stella was still with him over the phone. He was wearing green boxer shorts and a plain white sleeveless cotton vest. Both of his knees were pressed together and he sat on the couch with his feet up like a scared Bollywood bride forced into marriage.

In response to my entry into the guest room, Mr John let go of the phone receiver and placed it back over the side table. Then he put his feet back on the carpet in a feeble attempt to sit upright. He didn't wish to make eye contact with me and kept staring at the coffee table. Perhaps he felt embarrassed. Seizing the opportunity, I took a closer look at him.

Mr John had a slight boyish disposition for his age. But the youthfulness was confined only to his face while the rest of his body had seemed to age much faster. He was of medium build, had stooping shoulders and a slight paunch. His neck, chest and arms were covered with thick growth of salt-and-pepper hair over darkish skin. His naked feet were distinctly lighter in colour and showed off several warts, bunions and corns as a result of wearing closed formal shoes for many years. His hands were still clasped and rested over his lap.

Then Mr John looked at my face. He extended the palm of his right hand to offer me a seat on the two-seater sofa set beside him. He had a receding hairline, a big forehead and thick bushy eyebrows. Despite the petrified look in his eyes, he seemed to house a sound mind, something that I had feared otherwise. For a second, I was seized with doubt wondering whether Stella might have exaggerated the condition of Mr John while describing his untimely phone call. The fact that she was tired from working on a double shift fuelled my doubts further.

I sat down, cleared my throat and spoke calmly to break the uneasy silence, 'Thank you for offering me a seat, Mr John. I was informed that you wished to speak with someone senior at the hotel.'

Mr John clarified, 'I actually wanted to speak to the general manager. Are you the general manger, ma'am?'

'No sir, I'm afraid I am not the general manager. But I happen to be solely in charge of the entire hotel at this hour. I will try my best to assist you in every manner possible and solve any problem that you might be facing,' I assured Mr John in an empathic tone of voice.

Pause!

A few minutes later, Mr John requested in a feeble voice, 'Can I please have a glass of water?'

'Sure, sir.'

I poured some water into a clean bedside tumbler from the bottle of mineral water.

Mr John sipped the water carefully, still holding the glass tightly in one of his shaky hands, while pointing towards the wall in front of both of us with his other free hand.

'There! Do you see that?' He spoke in a terrified tone.

'Uh-huh. What about the wall, sir?' I enquired politely.

Pause, again!

And then Mr John continued, 'The painting that you see, ma'am. Those eyes in the painting can talk! They are alive and seem to follow you. Please take a closer look at it.'

I rose from the sofa to walk towards the painting. During inspection rounds on earlier occasions, my eyes must have glided over this piece of art at least a hundred times. I had probably checked the picture frame for dust or minor repairs, hunted for fingerprint marks on the cover glass, straightened it or adjusted the alignment of its picture light. I had never been asked nor required to comment on it as an art connoisseur. After all, it was an approved piece of work by the corporate art director of the hotel group. It felt awkward, being asked to stare at the painting.

As requested, I began to examine the work more intently. It was an abstract art form in oil paint drawn on canvas. Very basic hues of red, black and white had been used to create a female portrait. I observed that it wasn't a detailed or intricate picture. On an untouched backdrop of plain white, there were sharp outlines of matted hair, with unruly strands spread over the forehead of a sharp-featured face, resembling that of a middle-aged woman. She had a long neck and a revealing bosom covered with some sort of a see-through white clingy cloth. Shades of carrot-red smeared with a wafer-thin layer of white paint had been used to draw the well-defined tips over a sagging fullness of two heavy crescent-shaped breasts.

The subject flirted with various flaws of the human body. Tiny moles dotted her neck and a long scar had been slashed across one of her sunken cheeks. The apparently dry lips and square jaw were set into an apathetic expression.

'Look into the eyes, for as long as you can,' said Mr John. He looked slightly more composed now.

I took a deep breath and took a few steps backwards to gain a better view of the picture.

The eyes!

Yes, the large soulful eyes were indeed the highlight of the painting. It seemed as if the artist had spent an entire lifetime painting those deep eyes. At first glance, I noticed the black colour of the pupils and slightly greyish irises embedded in clean white eyeballs. The eyelids on the wide-open eyes had long and thick eyelashes. The eyebrows, on the other hand, were sparse. So far so good, I thought to myself.

A longer stare, however, felt hypnotic. I could not move nor could I redirect my gaze elsewhere. The powerful eyes held me captive and I felt I was being consumed by the painting. I stood there without batting an eyelid. Those eyes exuded an eerie kind of energy which kept getting stronger every moment that I gazed at it, till I felt that my mind was about to burst! My breathing had turned very slow and irregular and I could barely keep my posture erect.

Still starting at it, I stepped away from the painting and hit the edge of the bed. My knees buckled and I sat down. I moved my head to the right, then to the left; and then, I got up and walked a little distance forwards and backwards. A strong urge made me circle the room completely and it was then that I finally noticed it!

Yes, the eyes did follow me wherever I went. Unwillingly, I had completely submitted myself to the mesmerizing power of those piercing eyes. Was I faced with a soul-sucking inanimate female vampire? Or was my mind playing tricks? Had I been captivated by the dark forces of the night? I struggled with these thoughts like a scared child lying half-awake and alone on the bed, being haunted by the shadows of his subconscious imagination.

Still, I was unable to take my eyes off the painting.

It was then that Mr John spoke, 'Now, do you see what I see?'

His statement shook me out of my wakeful dream.

I took my gaze away from the painting at once. Although shaken to the core, I decided to quickly regain my poise and went back to the sofa. How could I have appeared jolted? I decided to stay in a state of soft denial for the sake of comforting the guest, saving the hotel reputation and, above everything, in a bid to protect my challenged sanity.

There was a cold stillness in the room as neither of us knew what to say.

After a while, Mr John spoke again, 'So, what do you think ma'am?'

'Ahem.' I cleared my throat and continued, 'You can call me Gauri, Mr John. I agree you could feel some discomfort if you stare at the painting for too long. I will have it removed from the room at once. I regret the uneasiness caused by it and I wish you have a more peaceful night.'

I stopped for a while and then said, 'Would you like to have a hot cup of cocoa or black coffee to soothe yourself? And I shall personally convey your concerns regarding the room painting to our general manager. Rest assured, sir, the general manager shall meet you first thing in the morning. We shall try our best to make up for the discomfort caused to you inadvertently.'

Mr John yelled back unexpectedly, 'Can you just drop your service mannerisms for a minute? Right now, I want to be heard, understood, comforted and reassured, not as a client but as a scared human being. Is it too much to ask? Lady, make no mistake. It is way below my dignity to extort complimentary services from hotels through petty complaints. You can keep that cup of complimentary hot cocoa to yourself. And that discount on my room charges which the general manager will offer me tomorrow can also be thrown aside, for all I care!'

Angry tears welled up in his eyes which he wiped away

with trembling fingers. After a few sighs and snorts, he drank some more water and leaned his tired shoulders back on the sofa.

Mr John spoke again with his eyes closed this time, 'I am truly sorry for the outburst. I fully understand that you must be just as scared as I am about the whole thing. All I can say is that I am not insane nor an attention-seeking narcissist. And I am not drunk,' he said and then, paused for a minute. 'Those eyes talk as if they belong to a soul still alive and trapped in that painting. Strange as it may sound, but those eyes remind me of my wife. There is a scary likeness between the eyes in the painting and those belonging to that of my late wife. She did not perish under ordinary circumstances, so to speak. She died a very lonely death.'

With each passing moment, his words sounded a little like a confession made by an accused undergoing a trial. As if he were unable to hold back his thoughts any longer and seemed to be at the risk of being devoured by them. He had to let them out!

'It was my absence that slowly led her into the darkness and killed her. It was her unending wait for me that engulfed her completely. I could sense something gravely wrong, but never expected that she would take her own life. I have stopped seeking answers elsewhere. I caused her death. Period! I have stopped believing the counsellor who says that it was her clinical depression that pushed her to commit suicide. I don't listen to my parents who remind me every day about the warning-cum-advice they had given me a decade before her death. They wanted me to end my marriage on grounds of spousal insanity. Towards the end, it became unbearable for me to watch her rot away because of her sick mind. I began seeking peace outside home, in my work and travel. But I loved her very much. I still love her. And, I miss her...a lot.'

There was silence in the room again. Mr John sat lifelessly on the sofa, half-asleep, with his head resting backwards. Understandably, he looked completely drained of his physical and mental vigour. I waited for him to speak again. But he lay there almost like a sick child resting with a dose of paracetamol after a long bout of high fever.

I didn't wish to disturb him. It was best to let him snooze a little with a security guard stationed outside, I thought to myself, as I rose from the sofa, quietly tiptoeing across the room. On my way out, I gently spread a duvet over him and placed pillows on both his sides. I also removed the painting from the wall, and took it to the hotel reception to store it safely until the next morning. I reminded the security guard to stay by the open door of Room 1408. I also asked him to alert me if Mr John wished to meet me again after waking up.

It was almost four in the morning. I dropped the painting at the reception counter and began writing the night log book. The painting incident at Room 1408 was a long story and it seemed to be, then, that it was still unfinished. I recorded the details of the event carefully. I left half a page blank to complete at the end of my working shift. With just three more hours to go, I raced against time to complete my pending duties.

Somehow, I had managed to compartmentalize the terrifying art mess of Room 1408 in my mind and decided to deal with it later.

At 6.45 a.m., most of my work was over except for the incomplete log entry regarding Room 1408. I was about to step into the lobby lift to visit the room when Mr John appeared from one of the elevators. This time, he was dressed formally in a business suit and Oxford shoes. He seemed to be in a bit of a hurry. Nevertheless, he did stop to speak to me, albeit very briefly. The security guard still followed him, carrying his suitcase.

'I was about to come up to your room, sir. I hope you are feeling better now?' I spoke with a genuine tone of concern in my voice, and added further, 'Are you checking out, Mr John?'

Mr John gave me a vague smile and took a deep breath. Despite the horrible ordeal he had undergone during the night, he tried hard to fix everything and look as normal as possible. He was clean-shaven, bathed and looked in control of himself.

'There's been a slight change in my travel plan. I need to attend to an urgent matter at work. I am flying out to Trivandrum just a day early,' he said and was about to walk away, but turned back towards me and continued, 'And, thank you for bearing with my eccentricity last night. Never mind that painting, dear! Goodbye.'

'When shall we see you again, Mr John?' I asked hopefully. It was a mixed feeling of not wanting to lose a customer and also to retain personal proximity with an interesting character in my otherwise mundane work life.

'Quite soon, God willing!' he replied and went to the reception to finish the formalities for an early check-out.

The security guard revealed that Mr John had woken up at 6 a.m. and walked up to him. He enquired about the time when I had left the room. He also handed over a generous amount of money as tip to the guard who, in turn, helped Mr John with his luggage, out of an overwhelming sense of gratitude.

Back at my duty desk, I completed the log book entry regarding the painting episode in Room 1408. I described how the lady in the painting had been perceived as alive by the guest and the extent to which it had affected him. I did not shy away from using words like 'haunted' and 'ghost' in the official log book.

However, I did not make any mention about my own experience with the painting. Perhaps, I was scared of exposing my fears to the people whom I worked with? Or, maybe, I felt too psyched out and ashamed to admit a paranormal experience? Nonetheless, I ended the note with an appeal to the general manager and relevant departmental heads to look into the matter more carefully, especially the painting. I also put forth a suggestion to perform a cautious examination of all paintings displayed in the hotel to avoid guests from getting scared in future.

Having completed my night shift, I quietly left the hotel. The only thoughts that lingered in my mind were sleep, sleep and more sleep. I yearned to hit my bed and take rest during the day to be able to work again that night.

♦

The waiting seemed endless at the general manager's office the next morning. I kept staring at my wristwatch every now and then. My mouth felt somewhat bitter and I struggled with a pounding headache. It was almost 9 a.m. and I had been asked to attend the morning meeting, in continuation from my night shift. I grew restless with each passing minute and felt bored and tired from all the wakeful nights of work and action.

I could also spot the painting from Room 1408 displayed on a separate side table. Anyway, the wait was finally over with a hurried entry of the general manager and various heads of department. I stood up to welcome the procession of senior managers, headed by their leader. The atmosphere seemed cordial as everyone in the room greeted each other.

After being seated, I expected the general manager to

initiate the discussion. And yet, he wasn't stirring. I could feel a knowing silence around me. Did I miss something? Why the pause—I kept wondering to myself!

And then, the office door was thrown open by an elderly gentleman. Each one in the room rose to acknowledge his commanding presence. The general manager ushered him inside and welcomed him. I had never met him earlier. Yet, I greeted him with the same fervour as the others. He was promptly offered a seat next to the general manager, but he pulled the chair towards the painting.

After gulping down a glass of water kept at the side table, the aged gentleman took a deep breath and closed his eyes. We watched him intently as if he was a soothsayer about to spell out a prophecy. I took a good look at him. He was dressed informally in a pink floral printed shirt which hung loosely over white linen pants with floaters on his feet. A flashy metallic watch adorned his wrist which he kept flipping awkwardly. His face gave the impression of mixed lineage, somewhat brown hair and hazel eyes typical of Portuguese descent. His thin face, with abundant wrinkles on unshaven cheeks and a large forehead, shone with wisdom.

A few moments later, he began slowly, 'Good morning to everyone in this room. I can recognize quite a few people here. But, some of you may not know me and that's fine since I generally work in my private office housed at the corporate headquarters. I largely deal with the projects team during the inception stage of an upcoming or acquired hotel property, much before the hotel begins functioning. I have been associated with the company for as long as thirty-five years now. My retirement from work has been long overdue but the promoters refuse to unshackle me from my duties, you see!'

There was suppressed laughter in the room which I politely joined in.

'My name is Salvador de Penha. But I prefer to be addressed as Salva. I happen to be the corporate art director of the company. My tryst with fine arts began as a small child while wandering on the streets of Goa, which is also my birthplace. Although blessed with a keen sense in appreciating art, I am not an artist myself. I have spent a lifetime consulting in fine arts, both sculpture and painting.'

As he spoke, I began to grow wary of the presence of the elderly art director. Had the poor old man been compelled to visit the hotel because of the stir created from my log book entry? Did I use too many strong words while writing about the painting incident of Room 1408 the night before? What if I am questioned by an art connoisseur of his stature to explain my humble yet outrageous take regarding the incident? I felt giddy with all these disturbing thoughts.

Without wasting any more time, Mr Salvador de Penha clarified, 'Today, I am here to respond to the observations made by one of the hotel staff members regarding a painting. I was given to understand that the painting of this lady displayed here…,' he said pointing towards it, '…alarmed one of the guests because of her moving eyes that seemed to be following him everywhere. Am I correct about the issue?'

'Yes, indeed!' I said.

At once, all eyes turned towards me. For a second, I regretted speaking out of turn.

'Were you the staff member present that night with the guest?' the art director asked.

'Yes, sir. I was on duty when the stir took place in Room 1408,' I replied, almost whispering.

To my relief, Mr De Penha didn't appear angry with my

fearless reporting of the matter and continued to speak calmly, 'Gauri,' he addressed me, taking a cue from my uniform name tag, 'Thank you for bringing the matter to our notice. I felt happy to be challenged for the first time in a career that must have begun even before your birth. Till date, no one has ever questioned a piece of art approved by me. Luckily, I was able to trace the artist and speak with him through the label number and corresponding catalogue. I am here to unravel the mystery for all of us sitting here.'

He cleared his throat and went on, 'If one was to read the hidden title on the back of the painting—"Did E-Y-E Lie?" with Eye spelled as in E-Y-E and not "I"—one would understand the uniqueness of this work of art. The eyes that have been drawn by the artist are indeed distinct from others. These follow the viewer from every possible angle. All it takes for the effect to work is to have the subject in the painting look straight ahead. The viewer's visual perception takes care of the rest. No matter from which angle one looks at the painting, the painting itself doesn't change. It's like looking at a flat surface. The pattern of light and dark remains the same. This painting technique is called the linear perspective, where all lines in a painting go to a common point and it creates the impression of depth and distance. Another example of this drawing technique is the world-famous painting of Mona Lisa.'

Everyone had gone silent in response to the logical explanation. But there was one more doubt in my mind. I mustered up some more courage and asked, 'But the eyes seemed to be alive and moving. They seem to hypnotize the viewer. How do you explain that?'

'Good question, Gauri. Have you ever held a steady gaze on the flame of a burning candle while sitting in complete darkness? Of course, the flame needs to be kept at the same level as those of your eyes and you need to breathe deeply and slowly in a relaxed manner.

'At first, your mind will probably wander with your restless eyes resisting all efforts to keep still. But something rather special happens when you look deeper. Gradually, you have no visual awareness of anything but the candle flame. This is a profound experience. Your eyes are open, but you are actually not seeing anything but the small flame in front of you. As a result, it feels as though there is no distance between yourself and the flame. In essence, you become one with the flame and it feels that the flame is alive. But when the flame is replaced with a pair of human eyes in a painting, such as this one, it appears to your mind as though the eyes are alive. And, if your brain is preoccupied with a particular thought, it manifests through the eyes of the painting. So, what the guest may have experienced is the manifestation of an unsorted thought in his mind. Did he mention any specific correlation with regard to the eyes in the painting?'

'Well, yes,' I said, 'He was reminded of his late wife who didn't die under usual circumstances.'

Then, I added cautiously, 'But why did I have a similar feeling?'

'Fear is contagious, my dear. Deep-seated fear infects not just the scared person but everyone around him.'

After a deep breath, Mr De Penha continued, 'I actually hail the artist despite the serious stir his painting has created. This is a very fine piece of art here. It is alive. It mirrors what goes on in our minds. These eyes have the capacity to exude limitless joy, if you look for happiness; can emit unending inspiration if you seek it; can give out an ocean of love if you are in need of affection. I strongly recommend that the painting be put back to its original guest room and maybe the particular guest can be assigned other rooms whenever he arrives next. With that, I rest my case.'

I had mixed feelings of being belittled and enlightened at the same time during the rest of the discussion. It was unanimously agreed among the senior management that the painting should be restored to Room 1408. I excused myself early saying I was tired as I had continued from the night shift.

As I walked out of the general manager's office, I stopped to gaze at a few familiar paintings in the lobby corridor. It was a fresh experience trying to relish the artwork rather than looking for dirt on the glass or check picture frame repairs. Each work of art seemed so different today...

Indeed, Did Eye Lie?

LOST AND FOUND

The hotel staff witnesses all sorts of belongings left behind by departing guests, an assortment of invaluable, valuable and not-so-valuable items. Among other common things, I have recollections of unusual lost-and-found items, such as huge jars of snake wine also known as *habushu*, self-shot pornographic images and videos by guests, and even caged hamsters!

It is always difficult to judge the value of such items. In the event that my judgement regarding their worth went wrong, the in-house hotel policies and practices did save me from losing my job, but it couldn't safeguard my existence against the wrath and desperation of these forgetful guests.

There were ample instances to prove that the value of any lost-and-found object could not be ascertained merely by its appearance, age, label or re-sale potential. It's the circumstances under which these lost items were found that determined whether they were precious or worthless, and in a few cases… err…avoidable!

Solitaire Ring from the Maharaja Suite 1701

I rushed past the heavily carpeted floor and narrow passage of the guest corridor to take a final glance at Suite 1701 when this frantic message scrolled through the tiny screen of my pager.

Guest in lobby. #1701. Needed urgently!

I hurriedly opened the door of Suite 1701 with my master key card and began my routine room inspection. I also called up the reception on speaker mode.

'Good morning, reception! This is Sonya speaking. How can I help you?' answered the receptionist with a stoic overtone in her voice. The image of a young, suave, charming and well-dressed woman flashed through my mind.

And then, there I was, scampering around the place in a ruffled sari with unkempt hair falling over my tired shoulders. I yelled over the speaker, completely out of breath, glancing at my dishevelled reflection on the mirror hanging on the opposite wall.

'Hey!' I gasped, 'This room was slated for an evening arrival. How did Mr Singhal arrive so soon?' I voiced my protest.

'Oh, that! We have a VIP walk-in arrival here. Mr Singhal's room booking has been shifted to another suite. But please clear this room ASAP!' Sonya replied coolly.

'This is not a standard room, Sonya. This is an elaborate suite with an even more elaborate inspection list. So, please hold your horses till I give a clear signal,' I said.

'Huh! Let me see if I can ask the welcome desk to make their arti, teeka and garland routine as elaborate as your room inspection,' she said, with a hint of sarcasm. 'But, please give me this room in not more than ten minutes,' Sonya said and hung up the phone abruptly.

A few minutes later, I had almost finished checking the room and was about to leave when I had a strong inexplicable urge to look under the sofa in one corner of the sitting room. I succumbed to this idea and bent down next to the sofa. I peered into the darkness underneath and saw a small shiny object lying in the farthest corner. I pulled it out and my body froze at the sight of what I had found. It was a shining rock set in a platinum ring frame.

A diamond solitaire? Quite possible, I thought to myself.

I stood there by the window in the gleaming sunlight trying to assess the genuineness of the solitaire ring. I was no connoisseur and found it difficult to come to any conclusion about the value of this piece of jewellery. Suddenly, the ringing sound of opening elevator doors reminded me of the arriving guest, the VIP who must be on his way up to the room. I quickly stored the ring in my diary pouch and rushed out into the corridor.

Phew! That was close, I thought to myself as the guest walked past me escorted by a guest relations executive and bell boy who carried a Louis Vuitton suitcase. I greeted his presence as usual and he responded warmly. He appeared to be rather ecstatic with the longer-than-usual welcome ceremony, blissfully unaware about the delay regarding room clearance.

Next, I rushed to the housekeeping office to alert my head of department about the possibility of having found a lost diamond solitaire ring. The in-house lost-and-found policies for such highly valuable items mandated electronic safekeeping with the departmental head, who was also the sole custodian of its access code.

♦

'Boss, I found this a few minutes back,' I said handing the ring over to Ms Malini Pande.

'Oh my! Look at that. Can you believe it? The guests seem to be getting richer and richer with each passing day. How can somebody leave behind a diamond solitaire?' she replied in dismay.

'So, you do believe this rock here is a diamond?' I cross-checked with her.

'I am as sure as I can be, dear! This is a diamond solitaire indeed. Just look at this beauty!' Her eyes gleamed with expertise as she twisted and turned the ring against the light of an office table lamp, exposing her own thwarted desires. So what if she did not have an heir. She nursed a longing to own such an asset, just for herself; a silent yearning for something that she could never have because of her middle class salary. As for me, such instances were like a glass wall, as I could see the luxuries but never touch them.

'Sure, boss! Could you please put it in your safe while I do the rest? I shall have you sign the register once this item's entry has been made,' I left her desk and initiated the formalities.

I pulled out the lost-and-found register neatly labelled 'Very Valuable' and opened the intranet screen on my desk computer. I began the hunt for the previous occupant of Suite 1701 by swiftly typing inputs into the computer. The room history section over the intranet revealed that this suite had been occupied by a couple named Mr and Mrs Tyagi.

Mr Anand Tyagi was a regular guest who frequented the hotel during his many business trips. Further enquiry into the system showed that he generally stayed in regular standard rooms, and the Maharaja Suite was assigned to him during his pleasure trip as a token of appreciation for his enduring loyalty to the hotel.

Quickly, I scribbled down Mr Tyagi's contact details from the computer screen. I noticed that his cell phone number was also listed, another luxury gadget marking the status of individuals in those days. However, Mr Tyagi could not be reached on his cell phone and so I sent out an email regarding the lost ring. I also typed and couriered an intimation letter to Mr Tyagi's address.

Since the item in question was a diamond, the operating rules mandated the information to be passed on promptly to the guest. Therefore, I decided to apprise him of the valuable lost-and-found diamond ring through the landline telephone number, the technology of the masses, as well.

I laid out the standard operating manual that contained the step-by-step lines to be communicated to the guests. I dialled the telephone number listed in the hotel guest history.

'Good afternoon, ma'am! May I speak with Mr Tyagi? This is Gauri calling from The Best-est Hotels. I work as a housekeeper here,' I introduced myself with utmost care.

A pleasant female voice had answered the phone.

'Um-hum,' responded the lady on the other side, 'Mr Tyagi is not around. You can tell me what this is about.'

'Thank you, ma'am!' I answered politely, 'With your kind permission, may I know who I am speaking with?'

'I am his wife, Mrs Anju Tyagi,' she replied.

'Oh! It is such a pleasure speaking with you ma'am. Mr Tyagi has been a frequent guest at our hotel and his presence is held in such high esteem,' I blabbered to buy some extra time so I could cross-check the name with the hotel information system on the computer screen. I gave a sigh of relief when the name tallied correctly. I was indeed in conversation with Mrs Tyagi.

'Thanks for your kind words, dear. But is this some kind of a sales promotion call? I am to believe that housekeepers have been made multi-functional at The Best-est Hotels and they perform sales calling as well?' Mrs Tyagi questioned.

'Oh. That's not the case, ma'am!' I went on to clarify, 'Actually, I just wanted to inform you that we found a diamond solitaire ring after you checked out of the Maharaja Suite yesterday. It was tucked under the corner-most sofa in the sitting room. It seems to be very valuable and is now stored carefully with us. Please advise us on how and when we can return the item to you.'

'Are you sure about this?' Mrs Tyagi replied in a surprised tone. 'As much as I am tempted to steal the solitaire from you, my dear, let me confess that the ring cannot be mine. Firstly, I never stayed at your hotel, though Anand was out on a business trip and might have visited you. And, secondly, my husband would have found out about the missing ring by now if he wished to present it to me as a surprise gift. He came back late evening yesterday.'

Then she added, 'It could belong to someone who stayed in the same room earlier. You could check.'

'Thank you for your time, Mrs Tyagi,' I responded, a bit confused. 'I am sorry if I wasted your time. It was such a pleasure speaking with you, ma'am.'

Even though I had disconnected the phone, somehow, I felt that the talk was not over yet. My mind started racing. Did the room assigned to Mr Tyagi contain the previous occupant's ring? Should I call up all the previous occupants of the room? What if the ring indeed belonged to somebody else? I panicked at the thought of my possible negligence in room inspection being found out by my boss. But how come the person who lost the ring never followed up? Anyway, I completed the deposit formalities of the ring and made an entry in the lost-and-found register that my boss signed as a proof of receipt. I was still worried and decided to defer the discussion with my boss until evening towards the end of my shift.

Still deep in thought, trying to figure out the next steps, I returned to the guest floors and started inspecting more rooms. A few minutes later, the housekeeping desk coordinator interrupted me with a pager message asking me to call back urgently.

'Good afternoon, housekeeping! How may I help you?' the desk coordinator, Vasudha, answered in a polite voice.

'Good afternoon, Vasudha. This is Gauri. You had asked me to call you urgently?' I responded.

'Yes, Gauri ma'am. Mr Tyagi had called up to confirm that he had received your email regarding the lost diamond ring from 1701. He also said that he will be collecting the ring personally on Monday. He thanked the hotel staff for being so prompt and honest,' she informed me with a smile.

Is this for real? I wondered, recalling the conviction with which Mrs Tyagi refused to accept the ring as one of their lost items. Is one of them lying? I thought to myself.

'And, Mrs Tyagi also called back right after Mr Tyagi hung up. She too was enquiring about the diamond ring,' Vasudha continued. 'I updated her about Mr Tyagi's confirmation call and told her that he would be here on Monday to claim the ring back. I also reminded her of our little interaction which happened day before yesterday when I had gone to deliver extra towels to their suite in the evening. She was sitting with Mr Tyagi on the sofa and had tipped me graciously.'

'What else did she want to talk about?' I asked further.

'Well, nothing much,' continued Vasudha, 'Mrs Tyagi hung up on me. She could have at least thanked the hotel staff. After all, it was a diamond solitaire ring! Anyway, let us catch up more on this later. There's a lot to do. Bye ma'am.' Vasudha disconnected the phone.

Secretly, I gave a sigh of relief that I narrowly escaped being questioned on my room inspection capabilities. But I felt more puzzled now. I tried to join the dots, attempting to think like a seasoned investigator.

Well, the suspense did not last that long!

◆

'Gauri, pssst...stop!'

Almost an hour had passed when I heard a voice from somewhere in the guest corridor during one of my final inspection rounds. I turned around to see Ms Pande hastening up to me. I stopped there, feeling the intensity of the situation in her walk and appearance.

'Ms Pande! Is everything fine?' I enquired quickly.

'Well! As a matter of fact, it is not. I am coming straight from the general manager's office and I am afraid there's some bad news for all of us. Did you call up the residence of the guest who lost the diamond ring?' she asked.

'Yes, I did make a call to Mr Tyagi's landline number taken from the hotel information system. But I followed the process manual steps meant for very valuable lost-and-found items,' I tried to clarify. 'Also, Mrs Tyagi could not recall losing any diamond ring although her husband confirmed that the lost item was indeed theirs. I was about to update you on the matter this evening. I still don't get it.'

'How could Mrs Tyagi have confirmed that the lost ring belonged to her when she was not even visiting us with her husband? Mr Tyagi was not with his wife, you see,' Ms Pande said to my utter dismay. 'Now, Mr Tyagi has called up our general manager and vowed never to return to our hotel. He feels that the hotel staff members harbour a very invasive approach towards the personal lives of its guests. He spoke at length and expressed his sheer disappointment over the call made to his wife despite his continued loyalty to us as a customer. And, from what I hear, he is not ready to accept any form of apology whatsoever!'

'Now, what will happen next?' I replied in a low voice, while gulping down air to relieve my dry throat in vain.

Ms Pande replied, 'Well! Let's learn from this mistake and review our lost-and-found policy. I have called for an emergency departmental meeting today at 6 p.m. Be ready with a detailed narration of the incident and let's brainstorm over possible amendments to the current procedure. We can't afford to make such errors in the future.'

Subsequently, it was revealed that my well-intentioned phone call from the hotel had caused a calamity in the Tyagi household. It was discovered later that Mrs Tyagi had for long been suspicious about her husband's philandering ways, but could not prove her doubts due to lack of evidence. Now, armed with sufficient proof against him, she had threatened Mr Tyagi under the guidance of the finest divorce lawyers. Terms like bankruptcy and defamation were tossed around.

Dazed and tired over the commotion caused inadvertently by me, I wished the day would end sooner than usual. I had had more than my fill of action for a day's work.

I watched Ms Pande take the elevator downstairs to the department and followed her after a while, pondering over the questions of 'lost' trust which would never be 'found' again!

Trust 'found' at the city garbage dump

I have vivid memories of that extremely hot summer afternoon. My heavily pregnant body struggled with another day of hard work. I was adamant that I would work till the very end of my pregnancy term, so that I could stay with the new-born for the entire span of my maternity leave.

It was hilarious to note the sudden onset of care and concern on the faces of hotel guests as my gigantic belly greeted them much ahead of a Namaste, handshake or smile! A few older female guests would gush over me in awe of my resolve to work while being almost on the verge of going into labour. And the suited-booted gentlemen would clear their throats in disbelief while pushing their bodies tightly against the walls of the elevators in order to accommodate my bulging body.

That day, I had barely entered the staff cafeteria for lunch when a frantic voice from behind called out my name, 'Gauri ma'am!' I turned around to see Vasudha, the housekeeping desk coordinator running towards me.

'Gauri ma'am, the CDs from room 1014...has someone thrown them away?' Vasudha asked and continued, 'The guest who checked out of the room yesterday informed me that he would be coming over to the hotel today evening at six to collect the CDs. He had left them behind accidentally.'

'I don't remember recording any CDs as lost-and-found yesterday. However, let me check with the room attendants who serviced the room,' I replied, recollecting that this specific room was part of a large in-house three-day conference booked by one of the leading multinational banks. The rooming list consisted of mid-level managers and senior bank staff, mostly local residents, but their stay was booked at the hotel for the annual staff retreat. The regional and global bosses too had graced the occasion.

'That's fine, Gauri ma'am. But please do hurry. It's already 2 p.m. and we are not even sure whether we hold the lost items. The caller sounded damn concerned!'

'Sure, Vasudha, I will get back to you soon,' I assured her.

Despite hailing from rural backgrounds, my room attendants were urban enough to see that the colour of 'gramophone record discs' had changed from black to silver, and had become smaller. Their seasoned eyes identified such digital stuff easily. Since there had been too many rooms to be serviced, the lost-and-found CDs must have been locked away in haste in one of their cleaning trolleys. I grabbed a quick bite and went back to meet the room attendants working on the guest floor. They did remember those CDs from room 1014 clearly; however, I was told that the items were found in the dustbin and had been removed along with the garbage.

'What?' I gasped in fear. 'How could you throw away CDs?'

My hopes also crashed into the garbage bin along with my confidence.

The room attendants retorted, 'Arre, ma'am! Please listen to us carefully. We are saying that the CDs were already in the dustbin along with some scribbled sheets. Why would we store items that were already thrown away by the guests?'

I left the conversation midway as it was not heading anywhere. I decided to contact the caller and dissuade him from coming to the hotel. I dialled the housekeeping desk and the desk coordinator answered promptly.

'Vasudha, could you please connect me with the person who had called up for the CDs? The items were disposed off along with the garbage yesterday since they were found lying in the guestroom dustbin,' I said.

Vasudha panicked and replied, 'What! Gauri ma'am, how do you plan on handling this? It is almost three o'clock.'

'I don't have any plan. Just tell me the name of the guest who called up and connect me to him. I will try my best to find a way out,' I responded while trying to cover up my anxiety.

A few tense moments later, the phone rang. I picked up the phone cautiously. It was Mr Abrar Malik, one of the probationary officers from the bank. He had a sincere voice and I mustered up the courage to speak to him in a peer-like tone.

'I hope you enjoyed your stay with us, Mr Malik? And

did you like the city and its weather?' I tried to break the ice with him.

Mr Malik answered in a casual tone, 'Hey! I like being called just Abrar. And, I am absolutely in love with the city since I was born here and still continue to live here my family. I stayed at your hotel only as part of the annual corporate retreat. But thanks for asking, ma'am.'

Then, suddenly, his voice turned serious, 'I sincerely hope you found my CDs.'

I cleared my throat and continued, 'Mr Malik, I am afraid the CDs were discarded with the hotel garbage yesterday since they were found in the guestroom dustbin. I am really sorry for your loss and would like to know what else we can do to help you.'

There was a long pause after which Mr Malik continued, 'I do not have the words to explain how crucial those CDs are to my professional well-being. All I can say is that my toil and sweat of six months has been trashed. This is my first job and unfortunately there's no back-up available. I probably threw away the CDs accidentally. Ma'am, is there no other way out? Is there a possibility that the CDs are being held at some garbage-room kind of place at the hotel? Please, please... you have to help me! In any case, I will be in the hotel lobby at six. And, if it helps to know the description of those CDs, please note that there are three of them, all labelled with 'AM' in pink-coloured ink, and packed in yellow plastic CD covers.' His voice was clearly shaking by now.

'Sure. Let me check one more time, Mr Malik...umm... Abrar.' I spoke with a newfound affection for the boy. I hung up while making notes describing the lost CDs.

I felt deeply concerned for him and wanted to protect his innocence since he had owned up to the mistake of throwing away those CDs accidentally. He could have easily blamed the hotel staff, just like many guests that I encountered in the past did. Well, he would soon learn some street-smart tactics, I thought to myself. But, right now, he definitely deserved some unconditional help!

I stormed my brains and prepared a neat flowchart diagram of garbage disposal steps followed in the hotel. Sequentially, the garbage moves from the guestroom dustbin → garbage section of room cleaning trolley → floor pantry dustbin → garbage sorting room → garbage truck of private contractor or the bio-compost plant → city garbage dump → finally, the waste management plant. Then, I began the investigation to locate the lost CDs in the hotel.

After an exhausting round of walk on the floors and making physical enquiries at the garbage sorting room, I finally faced the possibility of those CDs having reached the city garbage dump. My pregnant body was terribly exhausted by now and I decided to call off the garbage rescue operation. However, recollections of that hapless voice kept nagging me!

I went to the housekeeping desk and handed over my duty charge and keys to Vasudha.

'Ok, so here it is. Since 1014 needs help with his lost CDs at any cost, the city garbage dump beckons me! It could be more than six in the evening before I reach, so please tell Mr Malik to wait till I am back. Wish me good luck in my glorious expedition!' I said with a hint of sarcasm.

♦

I grabbed my purse from the executive staff locker room and quickly boarded one of the taxis at the hotel taxi stand near the security gate. Of course, the destination was our nearest city garbage dump.

The taxi driver was an aged Sikh gentleman, somewhat hefty. It was difficult to convince him before he finally agreed to drive to the nearest garbage dump. He kept staring at me from the rear-view mirror with curious eyes. Finally, he broke his silence.

'Madamji, pray tell me, why would you want to visit the garbage dump of all the places?'

'Sardarji, nothing serious at all!' I addressed him respectfully, 'One of the guests at my hotel lost some important CDs yesterday. We need to find those at the garbage dump. Is it still far from here?'

'Not at all, Madamji! We will be reaching there in the next five minutes. Would you also like my taxi to bring you back to the hotel?' he asked me with evident concern.

'Oh, yes! Sure. Thank you,' I answered back politely.

All my bodily senses were put under attack when I reached the city garbage dump. I saw young and old ragpickers moving around the rotting garbage and filth, sick barking dogs prowling, mud-coated pigs sniffing about, hundreds of crows pecking at the garbage, and vultures circling high in the sky. My ears were deafened with the cacophony of these scavengers and my skin revolted against a swarm of flies, clouds of dust and smoke from piles of burning trash. I covered my nose with a handkerchief to guard it against the horrible stench and started wondering how I was supposed to search for three tiny CDs in this vast expanse of muck.

'Do you need help, Madamji?' Sardarji shouted from a distance, where his taxi was parked.

'Yes, please. But, I don't know how you can help me,' I screamed back while wiping of sweat from my forehead. The summer heat was punishing.

To my astonishment, the taxi driver started waving a ten-rupee note at a group of ragpicker children. No sooner had he done that than a bunch of six kids with huge sacks hanging over their shoulders dashed up to him. Sardarji led the team and walked up to me like a seasoned sports captain. He asked me to describe the lost items and fix an appropriate reward for the tiny rag pickers.

I was unsure about the idea and expressed my doubts over the capability of such little kids, presumably illiterate to be able to find digital items like CDs.

The taxi driver understood my fleeting doubts and defended the ability of the young ragpickers and said, 'Madamji, these kids were born and raised here. They are our very own informal recycling army. Working long days and carrying large sacks, they comb through every nook and corner of the garbage dump site. This is our best bet! Do you have any other plan? You wish to look for the CDs yourself?'

I had to concede to Sardarji that the ragpickers were not just the best option but the only option we truly had! Thereafter, I explained the task of hunting for the discarded CDs to the kids and they bombarded me with several questions.

'What does the lost item look like?'

'How many items are there?'

'What is the reward money for the person who finds it?'

I pulled out a sample CD with cover from my purse and flashed it in front of the rag pickers. I provided a detailed description of numbers, labels and colours in the vernacular. After much collective bargaining, the tiny army of six children agreed to perform the task for twenty rupees each. One of the outspoken kids suggested that we sit in the taxi and wait more comfortably since it could take up to an hour for them to return.

Sardarji and I started walking towards the taxi. I was

overwhelmed with the unconditional help offered by the old taxi driver. For a moment, it really didn't matter whether or not those CDs could be found. Such joyful responsiveness from absolute strangers was worth the effort, I thought to myself!

'Do we have a fair chance of retrieving the CDs, Sardarji?' I asked the elderly taxi driver.

He smiled back intuitively with his eyes shining bright with wisdom, 'Yes, we will find them. Why don't you rest for a while?'

The view outside the car window was far from appealing and I decided to shut my eyes. But I could barely get any rest and wanted the suspense to end.

Several tense moments later, there was a faint knock on my window. I opened my eyes and saw the same outspoken child who had asked us to wait in the taxi. I stepped out.

'Did you find those CDs?' I impatiently asked the tiny army of ragpicker children.

There was no answer!

But one of the shy kids started to pull something out of the huge sack hanging over his shoulder. He handed me a newspaper packet. I opened the newspaper wrap and found three CDs labelled 'AM' in pink-coloured ink contained in yellow plastic CD covers. Yes! The little champs had indeed found the lost items. I felt overjoyed and thanked the kids.

Again, no response!

However, one of the boys extended his arm towards me with an open palm to remind me of some unfinished business. I took out the reward money as promised and handed it over to one of them.

Dart! The children disappeared as if they were never there. It was exactly 6 p.m. and I scurried inside the taxi and requested Sardarji to drive me back to the hotel as fast as he could. As soon as the taxi reached the hotel, I got down and signed the taxi duty slip. I also thanked the taxi driver sincerely for his unconditional assistance.

The walk back to the housekeeping department had never seemed so long before!

'Yay! The CDs have been found, Vasudha. Here they are.' I waved the item at the desk attendant in excitement as I entered through the door.

'Oh my God! I can't believe it, Gauri ma'am. How did you manage to locate such tiny items in the colossal waste of the city garbage dump?' Vasudha continued, 'By the way, Mr Malik is waiting for you in the lobby. In fact, he has already called up thrice from the reception desk in the past half an hour. Please hurry!'

I replied, 'Wow! I am sure that Abrar will jump with joy at the very sight of these CDs. Please make an entry into the lost-and-found register while I help myself to a glass of water, will you?' Vasudha attended to my request promptly.

After a while, I entered the opulent hotel lobby with the register and CDs held tightly to my chest. Despite the chaos and hustle-bustle of a busy evening at the lobby, the piano sounded melodious. The sight of roses and carnations centrepieces on the lobby was heavenly, to say the least. I approached the reception desk and asked for Mr Abrar Malik.

She pointed towards a gentleman sitting right across on the lobby sofa.

It would have been easy to locate Abrar even without making an enquiry. A boy barely out of college sat there anxiously, unable to find respite even in such pleasant surroundings. Giving hospitality protocol a miss and doing away with formal greetings of 'Sir' and 'Mr', I called out softly, 'Hi Abrar!'

Abrar jumped from the sofa and replied, 'Hello! Are you Gauri?'

'Yes, I am Gauri. And I have something for you here. See!' I flashed the CDs.

'Oh! Thank you, ma'am. Thank you so much!' Abrar sprang up with joy and pressed my hands together. He held them for a long time and only let go when he felt the stares of people around him. I decided to cut the melodrama short.

'You are welcome, Abrar! Could you please sign the register as a receipt of these CDs?'

Abrar completed the formalities and clutched the CDs tightly in his hands as if he never wanted to lose sight of them again. I took the liberty of reminding him gently about being more careful with his belongings the next time. Upon being chided softly, he kept whispering 'sure' and 'thank you' but stopped to make a sudden notice of my bulging belly.

'Ma'am, you went all the way to the garbage dump in this condition? How could I ever thank you? If there is anything I could do for you in the future, please let me know. I owe you really big!'

Finally, we exchanged our contact details and he left with a smile still lingering on his lips. I walked him to the porch where he got into his car and left. As I stood in the lobby staring at his retreating back, I realized that today, I had witnessed a trilogy of helpful strangers who had bailed each other out in difficult times.

By now, the hungry baby inside me had started kicking. Perhaps, a reminder for me to stop thinking about the dump and take care of my belly bump!

THE CHECKOUT

'Are you having your periods?'

Col (Retd) Dr Baweja tried hard to diagnose my ailment. His query had left me shocked. I struggled for words to tell him that I had been pregnant for more than seven months. Apparently, he had missed noticing my enormous belly. He had also overlooked my clumsy style of walking. He had even ignored my struggles to climb up the observation table. And the overstretched sari pleats of my uniform did not seem to bother him.

The fear of being incorrectly diagnosed by the ageing staff doctor overshadowed my pounding headache and back pain. I suddenly realized that I wasn't in safe hands. Horror stories recounted by the hotel staff came back to haunt me; stories about how a young maid suffered a convulsion after being administered strong fever medication on an empty stomach, how a laundryman continued working despite an ankle with a hairline fracture only with the help of some painkillers prescribed by the same doctor.

The medical room was also ill-equipped. It was a tiny damp hole at the end of the staff corridor in the basement that was created to fulfil certain obligations under the labour laws. The only time it was spruced up was during the labour inspection of the hotel. A day prior to the visit of the labour inspector, the floor was scrubbed, light bulbs were changed, and old bed sheets and plastic curtains were replaced with new ones. The aging doctor was asked to check the equipment and medicine inventory. He was also advised to be present for the entire day during the inspection, unlike the regular days when he would vanish intermittently.

I felt a strong urge to escape from the staff medical room. But it was difficult to offend an elderly doctor who had served the country as an army man. I was mortally petrified of the situation and finally decided to speak.

'Ahem!' I cleared my throat before addressing him, 'Col Baweja, I cannot have my periods.'

'Why do you say that, my dear? You are too young to hit menopause,' he responded while picking up the prescription pad and pen with trembling old hands.

'I cannot have my periods because I am pregnant,' I pointed towards my rounded belly, 'Seven months, actually.'

'Oh! You are pregnant,' remarked Col Baweja adjusting his glasses. 'Why didn't you say so earlier?' He seemed absolutely thrilled with the discovery.

I got off the observation table carefully and sat on the metallic stool placed beside the doctor's desk.

Col Baweja continued, 'Don't worry. Slight back pain is normal to experience during the final stages of pregnancy. Keep your feet raised up while sitting at the desk. Take these pills for headache. Rest well and eat well. If the headache persists beyond tomorrow, come back to me.'

'Thank you, Col Baweja!' I picked up my work diary, pager and the doctor's prescription before scurrying out of the dingy medical corner.

What a narrow escape! Never ever shall I pay heed to the advice of that co-worker who suggested the medical room visit. I went back to work. After a while, I began to get better and forgot all about the headache. The cup of hot tea might have helped too. The inspection rounds of most VIP rooms were over and I felt hungry. It was lunch time already.

I had barely served myself food at the staff cafeteria when my pager beeped.

Urgent. Contact housekeeping desk.

'Good afternoon! This is housekeeping,' answered the desk attendant when I called.

'And this is Gauri,' I tried to mimic the service mannerism.

'Gauri ma'am. You have a call waiting from one Mr D.K. Awasthi. He claims to be your close family friend,' responded Vasudha with no regard for my attempt at telephonic humour.

'Of course, I know Awasthi Uncle. He is a dear friend of my father and we are almost like family. Please forward the call here.'

The lunch room had deafening Bollywood music playing on TV and the crowd kept talking in high-pitched voices. It was quite natural for the hotel staff to unwind in the cafeteria after following strict service protocols for many hours.

The phone rang again and I picked it up.

'Beta, this is Awasthi Uncle. Can you hear me?'

'Namaste! How are you, Uncle? I'm pleasantly surprised with your call at my office...' I almost screamed over the phone to suppress the chaotic background.

I strained my ears to hear, 'Beta, you have to rush here. There has been a road accident. There's nothing to worry much. But your parents and sister need you.'

'What accident, Uncle? Where did this happen? When?' I felt dazed.

There was no reply from him. Or perhaps, I could not hear properly. It made me nervous. So, I hung up.

Soon, my husband reached the hotel to pick me up from work. He had already booked the earliest air tickets and we reached the airport in no time.

'What really happened?' I asked desperately. 'Why won't you tell me anything?'

'All I know is that there has been a near fatal road accident. Maa, Baba and Didi were in the same car. Even Awasthi Uncle and his wife were travelling with them.'

'Are they fine now?' I struggled to speak with a lump in my throat.

My husband put his arms around my shoulders and spoke in an assuring manner, 'I think so. We'll reach there soon.'

◆

Maa lay motionless.

I gave her the last bath trying to imagine my own first bath that she must have given me. I held her cold hands in mine for a little longer than necessary after washing them. Those hands must have rocked me as a baby, countless number of times. I stared at the familiar sight of her face, her eyes and her mouth. The stretch marks had not vanished from her abdomen. I reached for her feet and bowed myself over them, to seek her blessings. One last time!

I howled out in tears, 'Maa! Maa! Maa!' I couldn't hold myself back and my entire body shook violently. The baby inside me kicked hard. Once. Twice. Then another time after which I stopped counting.

'Calm down! You're hurting the baby,' My husband cried out. 'We have to take Maa to the crematorium. Please get her dressed.'

Her bare body rested on the ground. I draped her in the orange bridal sari that she had worn for her wedding. Then combed her hair and put vermillion in the parting and on her forehead. I dotted some kohl at the edge of her tightly-shut eyes.

She looked divine!

She was ready to go. I dropped at her feet again, with my eyes staring at her frozen face. Visibly calm from outside, I felt shattered within. Memories from my teenage years haunted me. I recalled every word of mine spoken to her in rage, each action taken to defy her attempts to discipline me and the phone calls that I deliberately missed to avoid speaking to her. I had left home at the age of seventeen for study and then work. Maa had stood outside my train window trying to hold back her tears.

'Gauri, my little one, I know you are not coming back home now! You are going for good. I bless you with all my heart. But never lose sight of the values instilled in you because when I am not there, they will be your guiding light.'

I had dismissed her heartfelt words as just another sermon. I was barely out of school and was in a state of excitement to start a new life.

And then, in that moment of final separation, I could have given anything to go back in time and take back all my harsh words and redo all my harsh reactions. The only memories that comforted me were the recent ones, when I had begun visiting my home as often as I could and also had my parents come over to my place. Maa was pleased with the little nest that I had created with my husband to welcome our first baby. She also felt a sense of pride regarding my profession after seeing me at work and meeting my colleagues.

A huge crowd had gathered outside the house to bid her farewell. The only ones who couldn't make it were my father and sister. They were still in hospital recovering from near-fatal injuries from the car crash. My father had remarked much later that it was better to hear about the funeral than to see it happen in front of him. He was right. It would have taken him his entire lifetime to recover from the haunting images of his beloved wife being dressed and given away to the relentless flames of the holy fire.

The last rites got over. Relatives and close friends resumed their own lives after a while. And I also returned to work a month later.

◆

'Why is your blouse wet?'

I asked one lady colleague who was undressing in the changing room. She had just finished work from the night shift while I was getting ready for my morning duty.

'This is breast milk,' she replied matter-of-factly. 'You'll know more about it soon. When are you due?'

'In a month's time from now,' I replied, 'Is it normal to have milk overflowing through the blouse? Don't you feel uncomfortable at work?'

'Of course, it gets messy. But, it gets worse for the baby back home. My girl is just four months old and longs for my milk the entire night. She doesn't like being bottle-fed.'

'Why don't you refuse night shifts? You could work half days?'

'Are you out of your mind? I will lose my job. My family depends on my salary. With two managers on leave and one pregnant, I don't expect any leave for myself. How will the department run?'

There was no fitting reply to her question. I saw her change into a pair of jeans and top before she rushed home while I began my day at work.

But something had changed deep within me.

After the bereavement, it felt ridiculous to read log books, assign staff duties and smile for hotel customers without a particularly joyful reason. Even the slightest of indifference shown towards people hurt me. I could not convince tired workers for a double shift any more. And, no longer could I cancel leave requests put forth by the junior staff. I dodged all attempts made by the hotel staff and even a few familiar guests, when they tried to engage me in conversations. I preferred doing desk jobs with as little human interaction as possible.

I wanted to do something that could soothe my state of mind, keep me busy, not just physically, but also engage my heart and soul. I longed for work that could be done in some sort of a meditative silence. Besides, I also felt worried for my unborn baby. I was not prepared to desert my child at any cost.

Thus, I quit working at the hotel.

♦

It was a warm sunny winter morning when I woke up. My baby girl generally lay awake for most part of the night and slept peacefully through the mornings. I loved to smell her. She gave out a mixed fragrance of baby oil, milk and diaper cream. I kissed her lightly on her forehead.

Her father also slept on, lying next to her. It was a weekend.

I tiptoed across the room and sat at the study desk, savouring those rare and peaceful solitary moments. The sunshine poured in from the window all over the desk chair. I sat there, draped in a shawl, and staring outside the window. The balcony had been left untidy from the previous night. I was too tired to pick up the toys and roll back the sitting mat. The pram was also parked haphazardly. Big and small clothes hung over the clothes line.

And then, I sat upright. A blank notepad was staring back at me...

A NEW CHECK-IN!

21 November 2023

Six years on, *Her Master Key* is still changing lives and perspectives.

An ordinary person with extraordinary experiences—that's how Gauri describes herself.

What began as her debut book, soon turned into a movement to highlight the daily trials of modest hotel workers in India. A global crusade began as famous travel writers and presenters featured the lives of hotel professionals ardently working to create and keep a world of glamour, even in the contrasting reality of the country.

She attributes the irresistible itch to have written her first book to the famous quote, 'there is one book inside all of us'.

Gauri continues to churn out straight and simple heartfelt stories...just like her modest residence where we met over coffee and home-baked cookies.

Some edited extracts from her interview:

Reporter: You have spoken about catharsis through writing. Why do you need it?

Gauri: Blame it on the stars, maybe! I happen to share my birthday (12 June) with a late holocaust author who wrote a diary to cope with an imprisoned life during the Nazi uprising. Although the teenage girl succumbed to death at one of the concentration camps, she remains immortalized through her book—a compilation of her daily diary entries.

Her Master Key is my diary!

Reporter: Which character from your book is most special to you? And, why?

Gauri: One and all!

Among the guests, Anand Tyagi 'lost' the trust of his wife whereas Abrar Malik 'found' faith in ordinary strangers. The scared Solomon John represents manifested guilt that resides in all of us in some form or the other. The antics of the sycophantic Gupta ji add humour into an otherwise boring setup of government-sponsored hotel events. The window cleaner Chotu is immune from any fear or danger since he doesn't have much to lose anyway. Shekhar Wakhloo, the bartender stands for a struggle to find stability in the precarious bond of an artist and the muse. Laloo and Mukesh Dandekar prove that the individual human character can be quite different from a mob character.

Reporter: Are the events as recorded in the book real? For instance, did the crow incident from *'Diplo-mazey'* really take place?

Gauri: It is hard to say where fact ends and fiction begins. There is always a little fact in the fiction that a writer projects. Likewise, the recorded facts are usually supported through fiction. But isn't it true for everything? Look at social media, research studies, business meetings or even a plain conversation with friends over dinner. Don't we as human beings constantly keep alternating between fact and fiction to project what we wish to communicate?

However, these stories are indeed based on true events,

albeit with a bit of dramatization to add reading flavour.

Regarding the crow incident, it would be in the best interest of all that I do not make any comment!

Reporter: Did you expect a successful film adaptation of *'Tender Bartender'*, when you first wrote it?

Gauri: What can I say! Except that the story did have a strong appeal for being adapted into a screenplay. The unusual plot of the struggle of a muse to overcome deeper longings for his artist, held the audience's attention well. Shekhar could never come to terms with the nature of being a mere artistic inspiration for Bhumija. He may have developed love for her during their long afternoon sculpting sessions, but there was never any scope for them to stay together beyond art.

How does a muse feel after the work of art is completed? Especially if he happens to get involved, emotionally or otherwise, with the artist during the process of creation. This aspect has always intrigued me. There is so much glory attached to the artist, but the muse remains unknown, at least in most cases.

Reporter: What about Bhumija? Did she love Shekhar back?

Gauri: No, I don't think so. Bhumija was incapable of loving anyone, even herself. She lacked appreciation for her husband and also her adoptive family. Her perception of relationships had been clouded by a low self-esteem. She felt incomplete without achieving bigger things on her own, like perfection in sculpting and recognition. And, she devoted an entire lifetime in doing just that.

However, she wasn't ungrateful in life, at least not in the aspect of art. During her later years, she pursued the cause of resettling the displaced youth from Kashmir. Perhaps that was her way of expressing gratitude to Shekhar Wakhloo, the Kashmiri bartender, and also her steady muse, who offered both inspiration and a means to express that inspiration for the creative artist in her.

Reporter: Last time you appeared in a magazine column on Chotu, the window cleaner-turned-entrepreneur. How does it feel to be an important link in a rags-to-riches story?

Gauri: Chotu always had the potential for bigger things. He was diligent, intelligent and fearless. And, he rightly deserved the entrepreneurial success. My book merely highlighted his case. As a result, help began to pour in from all ends.

The first came from Abrar Malik, now a senior banker, who secured angel funding for Chotu's start-up of housekeeping outsourcing units. He maintained the continuum of 'strangers helping strangers' on my request. After all, I had found those lost CDs that saved him from losing his job!

> 'My book merely highlighted his case. As a result, help began to pour in from all ends.'

Reporter: Is Solomon John still haunted by the hotel room painting?

Gauri: Not any more. He was relieved to read his story followed with the explanation provided by the hotel art director. It helped him unravel the haunting mystery.

He also practices yoga and candle meditation and has been able to attain some peace of mind now.

Reporter: Does the Sheikh continue being a pervert? Does Nouf still light the bakhoor lamp?

Gauri: It's hard to say anything for sure. We can only hope that he has mended his ways with women. But yes, things have certainly changed in their lives after the bakhoor was smashed into pieces. Nouf now lights a different lamp—'the lamp of change'. She writes books and columns to highlight stories of courage and hope for women. She also releases inspiring podcasts to blow winds of change in her society.

Reporter: I recently met Ambassador Hiten Mediratta who remarked upon how the book had personally impacted him. What do you have to say?

Gauri: I hope that he no longer feels awkward standing next to hotel staff while welcoming the government dignitaries. And that he also cooperates wholeheartedly with the hotel staff, during preparations, security checks and protocols.

Reporter: You have churned out heartfelt stories around your life in hotels. Then, why did you stop working? We would have loved to hear more stories!

> 'I could not cope with the tough working hours like many new mothers. The stronger ones lingered on! Their blouses would overflow as they worked till morning.'

Gauri: Yes, I am deeply indebted to my hotel background. It has given me everything—rich learning opportunities, lifetime experiences, a life partner and the book.

Nevertheless, it was difficult to carry on working in hotels after a baby. As clichéd as it may sound, I could not cope with the tough working hours like many new mothers. The stronger ones lingered on! Their blouses would overflow as they worked till morning. The husbands would often bring their babies at the staff security gate, waiting to be nursed during the wee hours. As for me, it was unacceptable to work night shifts, leaving behind an infant at home to be taken care of.

Matters got complicated further with the untimely death of my mother during the eighth month of my pregnancy. Suddenly, I had two babies to look after—an infant and a widowed father. Work had to take a back seat.

Reporter: Is it difficult to work in hotels? Please elaborate.

Gauri: Yes, it is difficult working in hotels. It is round-the-clock work and you are not allowed to crumble under pressure.

But our society is yet to come out of a feudal mindset and show respect towards service-oriented work, such as hospitality. The 'sense of entitlement' is so deep-set in our culture that domestic travellers seem to believe that they truly own the hotel staff as bonded labourers for the period of their stay. It is important to understand the work of hoteliers, whose 'services' are often confused with 'servitude'.

> '...our society is yet to come out of a feudal mindset and show respect towards service-oriented work such as hospitality.'

Wealthy industrialists mistake floor housekeepers for illiterate and underprivileged women vying for their wealthy attention. Or rich socialite Indian ladies, who are nothing but trophy-wives, scream at restaurant waiters during afternoon kitty parties. Such hurtful attitudes make it difficult for educated youth to sustain themselves at work in hotels.

Next, families, parents and youth do not seem to regard hospitality as a respectful career choice. I guess this also stems out from the same feudal mindset. But things are changing now.

Reporter: Why do you say that things are changing now?

Gauri: Slowly but surely, hospitality has gained wider acceptance in the Indian society. Not just as a career option but also as an occupation. The salaries and working conditions appear to have improved substantially. Only the smaller and genuine trade unions seem to be surviving in hotels as more and more work is getting outsourced to external agencies. There is better awareness among hotel leaders towards the working condition of female staff. It is not rare to spot 'in-house' crèches for working ladies. There is stricter compliance with maternity leave regulations and liberal views on helping new mothers make softer transitions back into work. The new age consultants, executives and second generation business owners have enough global exposure to treat hotel staff workers as equals. The domestic travellers have also begun to appreciate 'service' without 'servitude'—something that their foreign counterparts have always been doing.

Reporter: How different did you find the foreign travellers from domestic ones?

Gauri: Overall, foreign guests were more friendly and easy to deal with than the domestic travellers with very few exceptions on both sides.

I cannot help but recall one Mrs Bodenheimer, who had stayed in the hotel for almost eight months. She was accompanying her husband who was the regional CEO of Southeast Asia for one of the prestigious German engineering companies. The middle-aged Bodenheimers were slightly reserved but extremely gentle guests. They had very reasonable expectations from the hotel staff. It was heartening to witness such powerful and esteemed long-staying guests being so hands-on in their approach towards daily living, despite being assigned a fleet of hotel staff at their beck and call.

In fact, Mrs Bodenheimer loved to cook and had been provided with a microwave oven in her room. She also preferred to make her own bed and dust the room furniture. She even recycled the towels and never wasted any of the guest supplies. The shampoo and moisturizer bottles were found squeezed till the last drop, leftovers stubs of used soaps were stuck to new ones and food was eaten till the last morsel, leaving only clean plates.

Mrs Bodenheimer was also particular about service timings. There were specific times when the housekeeping staff could enter to clean the bathrooms, vacuum carpets or conduct thorough weekly cleaning of fixtures and furnishings. Mrs Bodenheimer rarely contacted the floor housekeeping and called only when she ran out of cleaning dusters, dish-cleaning liquid, dustbin liners, or when she wished for extra flowers in the room.

Further, her voice and expressions exuded same level of respect for the illiterate gardener as well as the seasoned sales manager.

One couldn't help but notice the sharp contrast offered by domestic travellers. The latter's room-stay would often be marked by multiple and, sometimes, unnecessary room-cleaning demands and loud complaints over the phone. Their rooms would have garbage strewn around despite the dustbins, faecal stains in water closets and, of course, the flooded bathroom floors from not using shower curtains during baths. Most of them also used a bucket and mug as an alternative to the bidet, without taking care of the dirty water being splashed all over the toilet seat and the floor around it. It was also common to notice heaps of soaps, shampoos and moisturizer bottles, sanitary napkins, slippers and towelling items missing from their rooms.

Actually, it was not this silent ignorance but the loud arrogance shown towards hotel staff that was more difficult to bear. The junior staff of the hotel often attributed this rough behaviour to the guests' newfound wealth and corporate status.

Reporter: You were sent a defamation notice by Best-est Hotels. The matter has grabbed wide media speculation. How do you cope with this?

Gauri: The legal battle still wages on!

Amid all the bitterness and media coverage, I am happy that an intense discourse has begun at various levels regarding the lives of hotel professionals. The hotel industry associations have made a serious note of the challenges faced by managers and workers. Even though the problems were long known, these never posed a notorious and threatening public exposure such as the book. The leading hotels have formed active working groups to deal with issues relating to women staff, migrant labour, and worker unions in a more systematic way.

The bottom-line remains that no hotelier can afford to jeopardize the future of Indian hospitality on account of its discontented staff.

But the publicity through the defamation case helped catalyse the book sales substantially. It was a blessing in disguise!

Reporter: We know that you are a Bengali from Bhopal. Tell us more about your background.

Gauri: My early years have been quite uneventful. I was no child prodigy but took pride in whatever little that I wrote. Even before my first book, I had stayed in touch with my passion for creative writing through personal and work blogs, newspaper articles and even technical reports.

My entire Bangla family, barring me, boasts of brilliant academic merits, best-regarded professions and artistic pursuits. Back then, it had been quite difficult for me to justify the choice of a hotel career to my close family and friends who were all either doctors, engineers, chartered accountants or artists.

Owing to some very unusual choices in studies, career and even, marriage, I landed up in big towns and metro cities at a very tender age. Still a gypsy at heart, I am forever in combat with my inner restlessness to offer stability to my brood of two girls and a husband.

Reporter: You just spoke about offering stability to your family that includes your husband. Doesn't your restlessness threaten the stability?

Gauri: Not if the restlessness gets channelized into joint constructive pursuits. My husband and I enjoy common goals and pursuits, be it raising our daughters, editing and selling this book or working on each other's projects. Meaningful tasks, respecting personal and work-related choices, are some of the ingredients that balance our potpourri of everyday life.

We had met at a young age and have literally grown up together. Our resolve became stronger after every setback; our celebration became livelier after every comeback.

In my experience, a balanced marriage is where partners help each other rise above difficulties and cherish a purposeful life together.

Reporter: Very recently, your elder daughter turned an author herself with her book release of children's stories. Did you

help her with the writing?

Gauri: Yes and No.

My parenting has been liberal without many academic and worldly expectations from children. Of course, there are boundaries such as time to return home by 9 p.m. for safety, respecting deadlines given by teachers, etc. But these boundaries are few. Both my girls are free to explore their interests in the wide pastures of free childhood. Perhaps, this has helped my elder daughter chase her dream of writing without getting distracted by conforming ambitions.

About her book in particular, my daughter never asked me to contribute a single idea, word, line or comment in her book. She has been fiercely independent in her writing endeavours so far!

Reporter: Any final words for your readers?

Gauri: You are my reason to write. I wish to continue nourishing your minds and souls with simple, straight and heartfelt stories.

Your encouragement keeps me going...

At one in the night, when the breath is slow,
I enjoy this dream to live and grow.

In this silence and darkness,
I feel a voice within,
'Gestation is over, you are complete.

Time to push hard, my dear,
Be born into this world,
so impatient to hear your first cry.

Your progeny has borne you for long,

nourishing you with her last drop of blood.

The chance to indemnify is here,
arise; break free from the umbilical cord.

May your lungs breathe till infinity,
your feet tread upon endless miles,
to prove worthy of the womb that carried you.'

I wake up once again,
to this strange yet kindling voice, sustaining my labour.

ACKNOWLEDGEMENTS

I am grateful to so many people:

My parents, for inspiring the love for creative pursuits in me.

Kriti and Chhavi, my two lovely daughters, for bringing a sense of 'gestation' into everything I do. I have learnt to accept that all good things need my time and sweat, if they are to happen!

Saurabh, not just my husband of seventeen years, but also a true comrade. He has read every sentence of mine so far, with patience and through the eyes of a hawk. A ruthless critic, he pushes my amateur random writings towards some sort of fruition. I owe my published newspaper articles and winning short story contest entries to his review genius.

Critics and readers of my personal blog, for encouraging my first feeble steps in creative writing.

Veneeta Kapur, my first boss, for toughening me up, so that I could face those difficult personal and professional upheavals. I always found a true mentor behind her seemingly authoritarian figure.

Prominent readers and some dear friends, for their sharp insights and honest comments: Subroto Bagchi, Tuhin A. Sinha, Ranveer Brar, Paranjoy Guha Thakurta, Karthika VK, Sesh Seshadri, Aninda Dasgupta, Vikram Harsha Annamraju, Rama Pisharody, Shrikant Bansal and Anupam Raghuwanshi, Puja Bajpai Pathak, Suparna Kundu, Geeta Bandaru, Abhishek

Kumar, Parthajeet Das among many others.

Shruthi Rao, my childhood friend, who was lost to the commotion of college studies, jobs, marriage and child rearing. And yet, while writing the book, I couldn't think of anyone else but her for copy editing, only to discover later that her best-friend gentleness stops at work. She is a widely published short story and children's book writer and also a stern editor. Well, thankfully so.

Finally, Rudra Narayan Sharma, my commissioning editor, for shaping up the book along with his mean team of copy editors, book designers and sales and marketing representatives. I may have nagged him more than others, with my silly fears as a first time author. Hope to do better next time!

Made in the USA
Monee, IL
03 May 2026

49438703R00105